THE WEDDING KILLER

Dr Hamlet Mottrell Series
Book Two

Michael Fowler

SAPERE
BOOKS

THE WEDDING KILLER

Published by Sapere Books.

20 Windermere Drive, Leeds, England, LS17 7UZ,
United Kingdom

saperebooks.com

ISBN: 978-1-80055-671-3

ONE

In the woodland clearing the air smelled of barbecued food as burning sausages spat and sizzled, gouts of flame flaring up as fat dribbled onto hot coals in the cut down oil drum resting on brick supports that served as a grill. The weather had been kind this spring and had spurred Dr Hamlet Mottrell into building the barbecue and bar area beneath the lean-to next to his cabin.

He had started its construction at the beginning of March, finally finishing it yesterday, his first free day in thirteen weeks following completion of the course he had been on. He had come top in every exam and to celebrate his success he'd decided to christen it, hastily phoning two of his friends, Alix Rainbow and Lauren Simmerson, inviting them to show off his barbecue and bar. But as he hurriedly turned the burning sausages on the grill he now wished he had done a practice run first. He was having trouble controlling the flames and had already charcoaled the home-made burgers, though his dog Lucky wasn't complaining as he scurried around his master's legs and devoured yet another overcooked chunk of seasoned beef in herbs, discarded in frustration.

'Having a bit of trouble there, doc?' Alix asked with a chuckle.

Hamlet half-turned, wiping his smoke-teary eyes with his forearm, bringing Alix's face into focus. 'A little bit of a hiccup, you could say, but if I can handle violent criminal psychopaths, then I can handle these little beggars,' he smirked back.

'You needed a little help with the last one, if I recall,' she said with a wink and pulled a sip from her bottle of beer.

You're not wrong there, he thought as painful memories tumbled into his head. Four years ago, almost to the day, his wife Helen, their unborn daughter, and the parents who had adopted him as a child, had all been brutally murdered. He had himself been found unconscious in the bathroom with his arm and wrists slashed. Medics had saved him, but in doing so he had become the prime suspect in their killing. And it had been Alix, the murder squad detective, who had arrested him and grilled him for days on end about their murders.

Thankfully, the only evidence the police had was circumstantial and they had been forced to let him go. But his freedom had come at a heavy price. His career as a forensic psychologist had been ended by the NHS Trust who had promised to support him, and to compound matters the press had pilloried him during the hunt for the real killer, making him headline news and dubbing him 'Dr Death'. Worse still, his remaining family, friends and colleagues had treated him as a pariah, a social outcast.

For months afterwards he had lived a life of hell; a mental blockage caused by shock creating a void about what had happened, and at the back of his mind there had been the uncertainty that he might actually have killed his family. In that time, holed-up as a recluse in his once beautiful family home, shunned by everyone he knew, he had come to the decision to move on with his life, and so he had sold the home he had made with Helen and retreated to live in the cabin in the 50 acres of woodland that his grandfather had bequeathed him.

And here he had taken up residence, mourning the loss of his much-loved family. In his darkest moments he had contemplated suicide, but the one thing that had stopped him from doing so was the determination to prove his innocence and see the real killer caught. And surprisingly, twelve months ago, after spending three years doggedly following every lead and clue, he had made a breakthrough and convinced Alix and her boss Lauren — Detective Inspector Simmerson — to open up a fresh investigation, finally clearing Hamlet's name.

'Congratulations!' Lauren's voice dragged him back to the present.

'And coming out top of the class, you swot,' Alix said, with a grin.

'What can I say? Some of us have got it and some of us haven't,' Hamlet returned, stabbing a sausage with a fork and slotting it into a bread bun. He held it out for Lauren. 'There's tomato and brown sauce there and some homemade coleslaw,' he said, pointing to the end of the bar.

Lauren took it from him. 'Looking forward to starting your new career?' she asked.

'Not sure "looking forward" is the right term. It seemed a good idea at the time, and I am genuinely grateful for the help you've given me, but changing career from psychologist to detective is quite a leap.'

'I wouldn't say that. You passed the course with flying colours. The trainers tell me you were the best interviewer they have ever had on the course. It's a natural cross-over for you, Hamlet. And let's be honest, after everything that's happened you're tainted goods to the NHS,' Lauren finished, biting into her hotdog.

'The boss has got a point,' agreed Alix. 'Not wanting to compound your hurt, but no one has come rushing forward to offer you your old job back. What better way of proving yourself? How many other detectives have got your skills?'

Hamlet forked another sausage from the grill, placed it in a bun and handed it to Alix. Then he got one for himself. Squirting in some brown sauce, he said, 'I know you're right, but I still wonder how my new colleagues are going to treat me. At some stage I am going to be coming into contact with the detectives involved in my investigation, and although they now know I didn't kill my family, there will be those who will have trouble accepting me as one of their own. And especially as I've gone through the new programme to become a detective without spending time gaining experience in uniform. There are bound to be some old school detectives who will resent that.'

Lauren swallowed her mouthful. 'Hamlet, you are going to meet a lot of sceptics and cynics over the next couple of years. You don't think I know what it's like? When I entered CID, sexism was rife. I had to put up with far worse than the snide comments you are going to endure, believe me.' Shaking her head, she continued, 'I know this is not going to be easy for you, but I have every confidence you have both the personality and the skills to win the cynics over. You have years of experience as a forensic psychologist and as a result you have gained a special skill set interviewing dangerous criminals.'

Hamlet looked at Lauren. 'That's all well and good you saying that, but you won't be around to support me when I have to deal with them.'

'Oh, but I will. Did you not question why all the detectives on your course were given their placements yesterday, except you?'

'I did think it was strange. But I just thought they hadn't made up their mind what to do with me.'

'I can assure you that is not the case. The moment you took up my suggestion to apply for the course, I had planned your career path.'

He furrowed his brow. 'Oh?'

'Yes. You will be pleased to know you are joining my team. From eight a.m. Monday morning Alix here is going to be your mentor and supervisor, and I will no longer be Lauren to you, but boss or gaffer. And I have my fingers crossed that your detective skills will be far better than your cooking skills.'

After seeing off their second beer Lauren declined the offer of a third, telling Hamlet it was her weekend on call and she needed to keep a clear head. Then, thanking him for a relaxing afternoon, she said her goodbyes and left. Alix, on the other hand, had no such restraints. She was having a much-needed lie-in tomorrow, she told Hamlet, and took up the offer of another beer.

There was still a good three hours of daylight left, and Hamlet suggested they take a stroll and finish their drink up by his favourite spot overlooking the stream that meandered through his wood. He had taken Alix up there many times since getting to know her as she enjoyed the peacefulness of the location. It was also a place where Hamlet did his best thinking.

Sitting down on the bench Hamlet's grandfather had built, Alix rested her beer on the arm and said, 'I've never asked you before, but why did you become a psychologist?'

Hamlet gazed at her. She was staring out across the stream, her dark brown hair pulled back from her face. 'Human behaviour is what interests me. The little grey cells,' he responded, tapping the side of his head. 'Why did you become a detective?'

'To make a difference. To help catch the bad guys who make people's lives a misery.'

'My reasons are not far off yours, you know,' he said. 'I also wanted to make a difference. I wanted to repair people's lives.

It started when I was a newly qualified doctor in A&E and I went to assess a young woman who had come in after an overdose. She'd taken most of the tablets she'd been prescribed for depression. It was a serious attempt at taking her own life and not just a cry for help.

'After they had pumped her stomach, I asked her why she'd done it, and she said it was because she couldn't have children. We got talking a little more and I quizzed her medically and she eventually disclosed that she had been abused as a child by an uncle.

'A year later she turned up in A&E with a gift of a bottle of whisky, wanting to thank me. As a result of seeing the counsellor I'd recommended, she had gotten pregnant. She later came back to the hospital to show me her baby girl.'

Alix turned to face him. 'What a lovely story, Hamlet. But why then choose to work in a high-security psychiatric hospital?'

Hamlet let out a hearty chuckle. 'I had this foolish notion that I could do something to prevent people like that woman from being abused in the first place, and to do that I first needed to understand why people abuse, so I took a doctorate in psychology and chose a job working with patients with psychological illnesses and personality disorders. I stayed in the NHS and later transferred to Moor Lodge, where, as you know, my life changed. Until then I loved the work. It wasn't all about dealing with criminal psychopaths. Many of my patients had complex mental health needs, and through a combination of medication and psychotherapy I was able to help them.'

'What about James Harry Benson?' Alix asked, referring to a former patient of Hamlet's who had finally been convicted of the murders of Hamlet's family. And who Hamlet had found out was his older brother.

'I now realise how little I knew about him. And yes, he is a psychopath,' Hamlet replied on a serious note.

'Didn't you ever have an inkling about him? A feeling about who he was?'

'Not until that night he lured us both to the children's home in Totley Brook. When he showed me all those photographs he'd kept, and told me why he'd killed my family. That was the first time I actually knew who he really was. Sure, I knew his history from when he was my patient. I knew that his parents were dead and that he'd been in that children's home, and I knew he'd had difficulties in his life that had resulted in him going to prison, but not for one minute did I realise his connection to me. My adoptive parents hid the truth from me. And James never revealed his true identity during any of my interviews with him. I realise now that he was playing with me. Toying with me like a cat does a mouse, and he murdered my family out of jealousy and revenge. And then he tried to kill me.' Hamlet's eyes fell upon the foot-long scar that ran along his inner left forearm. He lifted his eyes back to Alix. 'Sadly, James Harry Benson will never be one of those people I can help. He is, and will always be, a monster.'

'Well, you're a cop now, Hamlet. You can set out your stall to catch more bad guys like him.'

'I've already thought about that. Every opportunity I get I'll be working to put men like him away. What he did to me and my family has changed everything I've learned. I'm going to make it my personal mission to stop people like him harming others.' Hamlet turned away, his gaze settling upon the rippling water. Not a day had gone by since the attack by Benson at the children's home when Hamlet hadn't thought how different things would have been had Alix not been there. She had saved his life. Now it was his turn to do the same for others.

For the next hour, Hamlet asked questions of Alix about what his new role would be, what the team was like and the nature of the work he was likely to be involved in. When they had finished talking the sun was just dipping behind the trees, its warm golden light shimmering over the stream. In another hour it would set upon the two large upright stones on the opposite bank, the last remaining blocks of the ancient stone circle that was once part of a Neolithic burial chamber from 4,000 years ago.

For Hamlet, who enjoyed many evenings watching this amazing spectacle of nature, it was yet another reminder of why he had decided to make this place his home.

Alix pushed herself up from the bench. Picking up her empty bottle, she said, 'Thanks for that, Hamlet. It was a lovely barbeque. I feel so chilled when I'm here. It's a great place to switch off.' Then, with a chuckle, she added, 'I might just suggest to the boss we have our training days here in future. Catch you Monday morning, bright and early, partner.'

That night Alix lay in bed, wishing sleep would come. For the last two hours she had been listening to the noises outside; a couple of small groups making their way home from the pub, and the odd vehicle passing down the road, the headlights travelling across the ceiling.

Being close to Hamlet again that afternoon had triggered some dark memories. Whilst she had been sat beside him on the bench, she'd gotten a flashback of the horrific crime scene at his family home four years ago. The vision of his blood-splattered wife, her womb ripped open, visited her again in fast-speed, causing a tightness in her chest that had made her catch her breath.

She frequently suffered flashbacks from the crime scenes she had worked. They came at the most inopportune moments, a night out with friends, a birthday, or wedding, spoiling the event, until she chased them away with drink.

The other thing that worried her was the secret she had divulged to Hamlet about the brutal rape she had experienced as a teenager. He had got her to talk in a way that only her counsellor had done previously and that made her feel vulnerable. And yet, strangely, being in his company also excited her.

Regardless of what emotions he brought on she knew that for the next two years she was going to have to cope with them. Letting out a heavy sigh, she turned over, pulled up the duvet and closed her eyes, hoping the nightmares would stay away.

TWO

In the car park of Sheffield's Major Investigation complex Hamlet sat in his Range Rover, running his hands around the steering wheel, staring at the glass fronted entranceway to his new workplace, wondering if he had made the right decision. It was 7.30 a.m. There were only half a dozen other cars parked up. *Still time to back out.*

In the palm of his right hand he held the pound coin that would cast his future. He gazed down at it. Heads determined he should go for it. Tails decided he should leave now, return back to the solitude of his cabin and keep applying for psychologist posts. He placed it ready to toss, holding his breath.

Suddenly, behind, a horn blasted, making him jump, and the coin fell from his thumb. He spun around to look through the rear window. Parked behind was Alix, waving at him from the front seat of her black Audi. A wide grin was plastered across her face. He couldn't help but smile back. Alix had that effect on him.

His thoughts instantly spiralled away. He had been through many trials with Alix these past few years, and he had once hated her for what she had put him through. But the more time he had spent in her company the more he had grown to admire her, and since she had saved him from the clutches of James Harry Benson, he had become very fond of her. So much so, that when Lauren had told him at the barbeque that Alix was going to be his mentor for the next two years he had been thrilled. The only trepidation had been how his other new colleagues would receive him.

As that thought once again stirred in his mind, he couldn't help but wonder how the coin had fallen. He decided not to look. *This is my fate*, he told himself as he pushed open the car door.

'Nervous?' Alix asked, pulling out her jacket and bag from her car.

Hamlet couldn't help but observe how she cut quite a figure in her dark blue fitted suit. It immediately made him conscious about his own attire. That morning, after much deliberation, he had chosen a light grey shirt and dark grey suit to blend into the background. Though something told him that he wouldn't be able to do that.

'More than my first day as a junior doctor,' he answered, coughing to dislodge the lump in his throat.

Alix let out a light laugh, quickly looked him up and down again and then turned towards the building. 'Now don't slouch, doc, and follow me.'

Setting off after her, he couldn't help but smile. 'You sound exactly like my mum on my first day at school.'

Alix buzzed them through the doors with her electronic pass, guided Hamlet past an empty reception and up the back stairs to the second floor where the Major Investigation Team (MIT) was housed. Alix swiped them through another set of doors and along the corridor to the first office on the left.

The room was as he remembered it, large and brightly lit, with a dozen desks placed in groups of two facing one another but with chest-high workstation divides so each detective had their own pod. At the front of the room were two huge interactive whiteboards.

Alix led him across the carpeted floor to a pair of desks next to a window. The desk facing him was littered with paperwork with several files leaning against a desktop computer. He could just make out a keyboard.

'This is us,' she said, dumping down her bag on the cluttered desk. There was a photograph next to her monitor. It was a shot of her younger self in a cap and gown, huge self-congratulatory grin on her face, standing between a middle-aged couple. Her parents.

'And that's yours,' she added, pointing over the divide. 'Make yourself at home. And don't worry about the files on there, I'll sort them. Just put them on the floor for now. It's a case we finished just last week. I'll take you through it once we get sorted. It'll be the best way of showing you how we turn the evidence into a prosecution case. You can help me put the file together.'

Hamlet stepped up to his new desk. There were half a dozen folders on his workspace, and scooping them up he placed them carefully on the floor. Looking around he asked, 'Where is everyone?'

Alix was booting up her computer, watching it go through its loading process. She had removed her jacket and draped it across the back of her chair and was adjusting her lanyard over the front of her white blouse. 'Most of them will be down in the canteen, grabbing something to eat. I'm usually doing the same but I set the alarm early and managed to grab something before coming in.' She looked up at him and smiled. 'Got to set a good example to my probationer on his first day.' She returned her eyes to the screen and started jiggling her mouse. 'A bit of advice, Hamlet. Always have a good breakfast, and whenever you get the opportunity for a drink, take it, because you never know when you might get the next opportunity in this job. The other thing, and the most important of all, is you need to know where the kettle is.' She pointed across the room to a set of filing cabinets on top of which sat a kettle surrounded by many mugs. 'Your first job every morning is to make sure your sergeant gets her coffee fix. Savvy?' she said with a grin.

'Noted.' Hamlet slipped off his jacket, dropped it onto his chair and was just about to make his way across the room to switch on the kettle when she said, 'Seeing as it's your first day you get a pass this morning. We'll wait for the others to come.'

Hamlet nodded and sat down at his desk, opening the top drawer. A couple of biros rolled forward. Other than the pens it was empty. He was about to check the next drawer when a man and woman came into the office. He instantly recognised them, and judging by the return glances they recognised him. The woman offered a slight smile but the man just fixed him with a steely gaze. He remembered the man was called Nate but he couldn't recall the woman's name. They had both been hostile and given him a hard time during one of his many interviews in custody. Nate in particular.

As Nate headed towards his desk, he never shifted his eyes from Hamlet.

'Morning you two,' Alix said, looking up only briefly before returning her eyes to her computer. 'You know Hamlet, don't you? It's his first day. Do us a favour, Nate, stick the kettle on and make us all a brew.'

As Nate headed over to the filing cabinets Hamlet noted the not-too-pleased look the detective returned, and breaking his stare he pretended to go through his empty drawers as if he was busy arranging them.

More detectives filed into the room, all of them acknowledging Hamlet with either a brief nod and a smile or a kindly sounding 'morning' that made him feel a lot more at ease. Despite the frosty reception from Nate, the coffee he handed Hamlet looked the way he liked it and he made a point of thanking him as he made his way back to his desk. Hamlet then drifted his eyes over the divider where he saw Alix was still toying away busily on her keyboard. He wondered how long she was going to be when into the office strode Lauren Simmerson.

As she headed toward the interactive whiteboards, Hamlet reminded himself that from today she was his boss and he mustn't make the mistake of addressing her by her first name anymore.

The chatter in the office muted away, Alix stopped typing and everyone's eyes followed the DI as she picked up a remote and targeted the right-hand board. It flashed alive and a montage of images projected onto the screen behind her. Hamlet rapidly danced his eyes from image to image, storing them to memory. Two of the pictures were head and shoulders selfies of a pretty dark-haired woman who looked to be in her early twenties. Alongside that was an image of a street scene made up of large stone built Victorian buildings running the length of the road each fronted by a waist-high stone wall, a few parked cars the only sign of life. That is with the exception of a policeman in a high-vis jacket standing at the end of one of the driveways behind blue and white crime scene tape that was strung across the road.

A third picture showed a pink mobile phone with a broken screen and a card driving licence displaying the same face as the selfies. He read the name on the licence. Hayley Stevenson. Hamlet studied the series of pictures knowing these were a record of a real incident. His first case, and on his first day. An instant rush of adrenaline coursed through his body.

'Heads up, everyone. Can you give me your full attention for the next twenty minutes?' said Lauren. 'Before we start, I want everyone to welcome Dr Hamlet Mottrell to our team. I don't think introductions are necessary. Many of you already know Hamlet because he helped us to catch James Harry Benson. Regardless of what happened in the past, he's one of us now, so I want everyone to make him feel welcome and treat him like a member of the team. Okay?' She paused and eyed her squad, making sure she had their full attention. After quickly hopping her gaze to each and every one, including Hamlet, to whom she delivered a pleasant smile, she continued, 'Right, small talk over, now let's get on with the briefing. Mobiles off or on silent please. You know the drill.'

Hamlet studied Lauren as she waited for the detectives to finish messing with their phones. He couldn't help but think she had a presence about her that commanded attention.

'Right. We have a vulnerable missing person, twenty-one-year-old Hayley Stevenson, which the DI at Snig Hill has asked us to look at for reasons which I'll explain in a moment,' Lauren began. 'Hayley was last seen by friends at the Students' Union pub, Bar One, in Sheffield on Saturday evening. She left there just before midnight, telling them she was going to grab a taxi and go home. She lives with her parents and younger sister just off Herries Road near the Northern General. She never arrived home.

'Yesterday morning a young woman found Hayley's damaged phone and her driving licence on Northumberland Road, which is a short distance from Bar One, and she put a post on Facebook about it. That post was brought to the attention of Hayley's younger sister Rebecca, who calls herself Becca on Facebook, who had already messaged Hayley a few times as to her whereabouts and also tried to call her without response.

'Becca contacted the finder of her sister's mobile and went round to her home with her father to pick it up. When they saw the damage to it, which you can see on screen, and learned the finder had discovered it at the side of the road, they immediately contacted both the Northern General and the Hallamshire hospitals to see if Hayley had been involved in an accident.

'When neither of the hospitals had record of her admission the father contacted the police. Officers have spoken with the family and with the three friends she was with on Saturday night. The friends confirm that Hayley was with them from 9 p.m. on Saturday evening until just before midnight when she told them she'd had enough to drink and was going to get a taxi and go home.

'The friends say that although Hayley had had a few drinks, she was not drunk. Their meeting up was a routine Friday or Saturday night thing and has been for a couple of years. They are all at Sheffield University together in their last year of study. The three friends share a house together near Bramall Lane because they are not from Sheffield, and Hayley has crashed there on a few occasions but more often she gets a taxi home after a night out.

'The friends are firmly of the opinion that Hayley intended going straight home. In fact, she did mention to them that she was looking forward to having a lie-in and chill day on Sunday. Hayley has never gone off-grid before. She is very close to her family and especially her sister Becca, who is two years younger. It is that closeness that has resulted in Becca disclosing something to officers that has upgraded Hayley's missing status.

'Becca told officers that Hayley had confided in her a few weeks ago that she had received a number of calls from a man who just kept saying something similar to "I know you want me," before hanging up, and that she had blocked two numbers he had called her from.

'It would appear Hayley's parents weren't aware of this, because as soon as her father heard about them, he told officers about an incident that happened at their home two weeks ago that may or may not be linked. Apparently, the security light went on one evening and he looked out of the kitchen window but saw nothing. However, the next morning he found a bunch of wild flowers, bound by ribbon, on the lawn, and although he mentioned it to his wife, he didn't tell his daughters. These two things might be quite innocent, but combined with Hayley's sudden disappearance I think you will agree it is a matter of concern and warrants some attention.' Lauren lowered the remote and looked around the room. 'So guys, this is what we have. A twenty-one-year-old university student who was last seen just before midnight on Saturday and hasn't been seen or heard of since and also a series of crank calls to her mobile and flowers left a fortnight ago by an unknown person at the home she shares with her family.

'I know that under normal circumstances a missing person case doesn't come to us, but on this occasion the DI at Snig Hill has also raised similarities to the disappearance of twenty-year-old Jessica McKenna, who you may recall vanished eighteen months ago after an evening out with friends.

'She was last seen getting off the Supertram at the Cricket Inn Road stop at Wybourn, not far from her home, but she never arrived. She had also disclosed to friends that she had received several phone calls from a man who had said something along the same lines as the calls to Hayley, and on the evening of her disappearance she told one of her friends that she thought she was being followed.

'As you are aware, because some of our team were involved in that enquiry for a while, Jessica's disappearance was given loads of airtime on the local news and plenty of publicity but nothing of significance came up and she is still missing.' Lauren set down the remote and said, 'Questions?'

'Are we looking at a possible kidnapping, boss?' The question came from the woman Hamlet had recognised.

'Good question, Katie. We can't rule out abduction at this stage, and given that there are some similarities, the crank phone calls from an unknown man before Jessica McKenna disappeared, it is a likely scenario. However, I don't want that leaking out until we do a lot more enquiries and we take a look at Jessica McKenna's case again. With regards the question of Hayley being kidnapped, whilst it has been a line of enquiry, there hasn't been a ransom demand and I don't anticipate one. Her dad is a lorry driver, her mum works at a care home; neither of them have a large amount of money, and they live in a rented house. We will be speaking with them again today, and I don't want to heighten their fears more than they already are, so our public focus will be on their daughter's unexplained disappearance until enquiries tell us otherwise.'

THREE

Alix set off at the green light, edging into the busy road, joining yet another strand of slow-moving traffic heading out of . Sheffield in the direction of the Northern General hospital. Sat next to her was Hamlet. They had been given the task of visiting Hayley Stevenson's family to find out more about the crank phone calls to their missing daughter.

As they crawled bumper-to-bumper, Hamlet studied the documents Alix had handed him to complete during their interview, dragging his eyes over the many blank fields that required filling in.

Cursing beneath her breath as she stopped for yet another red light, Alix reached across and stabbed a finger over the paperwork. 'That's what we refer to as the victimology document. We get details of the victim's background and history and their associate networks. I guess you know all about that from your previous work. That gets handed to our HOLMES team, who input the information into the database. You know all about HOLMES?'

Hamlet nodded. The Home Office Large Major Enquiry System (HOLMES) was a computer database designed to aid investigations into large-scale enquiries.

'It's a painstaking job inputting it all, but it's worth it. The cross-referencing and searches HOLMES does reaps rewards, especially when there are cases that may be linked, like this one.'

'It's interesting that you refer to these as victimology documents,' Hamlet said. 'In my field, victimology is the study of why people become victims. For instance, during the

Yorkshire Ripper era there was the theory that the behaviour of the prostitutes who were murdered facilitated their own victimisation. This paperwork shouldn't be referred to as a victimology document.'

Alix turned her head sharply, before returning her gaze to the road. 'All right, smart arse. Though can I suggest you don't go challenging everything we do just yet. At least wait until you've got your feet under the table. It might not go down too well with the hierarchy.'

Hamlet let out a short laugh. 'Just saying, that's all. I'll keep my mouth shut and not embarrass anyone.'

Alix left the lights, spinning the steering sharply, turning onto a less congested road in the direction of the hospital where she opened up the car, pressing Hamlet back in his seat with the sudden acceleration. 'One thing you'll quickly learn about driving in Sheffield is it's a nightmare. When you get the chance to put your foot down, go for it. It's a great stress-reliever.'

Hamlet chuckled as he saw the lights ahead turn from amber to red.

The Stevensons lived on a 1950's council estate up a steep incline, with narrow roads and tight bends that made driving difficult, bringing about more curses from Alix. Even at this time of day the streets were clogged with cars, many having to park half on the pavement, and it took a little driving around until they found a spot in a nearby side street from where they made their way back to the house on foot.

Mr Stevenson answered the door. He was a portly man in his mid-forties, with close cropped hair and glasses. Alix showed him her ID and he let them into the house, guiding them through into the lounge where Mrs Stevenson was sat in an armchair. Their daughter, Rebecca, was next to her, perched on the arm of the chair, the pair clutching each other's hands. Mr Stevenson offered Hamlet and Alix the empty sofa and sat down on the other armchair.

Alix introduced herself and Hamlet and said, 'I know you have already spoken with a lot of officers, and I am going to possibly repeat a lot of those questions this morning, but I want to reassure you that it doesn't mean we don't know what we are doing. Hayley's case has been passed to our team and we will be doing everything possible to find her.

'Let me bring you up to date with what we have done so far and what will be happening from now on. We have spoken with each of the friends she was with on Saturday night, and we know that you have done the same. We have contacted the main taxi companies that operate around Sheffield, especially the ones we know Hayley regularly uses. One of those did take a call from her shortly after 11.30 p.m. asking to be picked up at the end of Northumberland Road by the Doctor's Orders pub at midnight. A cab did turn up, but it was slightly late at seven minutes past and she wasn't there. It hung around for a minute but when she didn't show up it went on to the next fare. We will be talking to smaller cab companies to see if they picked up Hayley instead.

'We have also started going through CCTV. We have a sighting of Hayley leaving the Students' Union bar just before midnight and it shows her walking up towards the Doctor's Orders pub. We are now checking for CCTV around the location of Northumberland Road as we know she was there for a time, because her mobile and driving licence were found there the next morning. What we don't know yet is what happened once she got there. And there are no other sightings of Hayley after she left Bar One on Saturday night.'

Mrs Stevenson's eyes glassed over and her mouth started to quiver.

Alix softened her voice. 'That doesn't mean there aren't sightings of your daughter. It just means that, for now, we haven't found any yet. There are a lot of cameras around that area and we have a team going through all the footage. It could take some time. Our enquiries are really at a very early stage, Mrs Stevenson, but as I said earlier, you can rest assured we will be doing everything we can to find out what happened to Hayley once she left the pub, and we will be in regular contact to update you.

'Our visit this morning is all about finding out more about Hayley which may help us discover the reason for her disappearance or where she might be. We want to know about her habits, who she sees regularly, what she normally does with her days and where she goes as routine. We also want to talk about the phone calls she received on her mobile that made her so uneasy, and also more about that incident in your garden when the flowers were left.'

'Do you think the man who phoned Hayley had something to do with her disappearance?' asked Mr Stevenson.

'Honest answer is we don't know. We have our technicians going through Hayley's mobile in the hope we can trace the person who made those calls. The fact that it's been damaged has made things slightly difficult but it is being done as a priority. For now, we just want to know more about the calls.' Alix looked across to Rebecca. 'I understand she confided in you about those calls?'

Rebecca started to speak but a lump in her throat caught her words and she coughed.

Her mum gave her hand a squeeze. 'It's all right, love. Just tell them what you told us.'

Rebecca gave a meek smile before saying, 'It was about a month ago now. Hayley was getting ready to go out. I can't remember the day. I'd just gone up to the bathroom and Hayles was in her room putting some stuff into her backpack. She was dressed as if she was going out but it wasn't the weekend so I asked her where she was off to. She said she was meeting up with some mates down at the halls to go through some work she had to do. That's when her phone went. She picked it up, looked at it for a second and then answered it like it was one of those cold calls you get asking you about an accident you've been involved in. You know what I mean?' Rebecca looked at Alix who nodded back. 'She listened for a few seconds before she said "F off weirdo" and hung up. She said the full F word though. I asked her who that was and she said, "This weirdo keeps phoning me and saying weird stuff. I've blocked him twice." I asked her what like, and she said he just kept saying "you want me" and she then said, "as if," and laughed. I made a joke about it being a secret admirer. Then she got ready and left.'

'Hayley never said if she knew who it was then?' Alix asked as Rebecca paused.

'No. But I got the impression she didn't know.'

'Okay. Did you witness her getting any more calls? Or did she say anything about any further calls to you?'

Rebecca shook her head. 'I made a joke to her a few days later about receiving phone calls from her secret admirer, and she said "I think the idiot has finally got the message".'

Alix nodded. 'Thank you for that, Rebecca.' Then she looked to Mrs Stevenson. 'And as I've said, we will be going through Hayley's phone to see if we can trace the caller. Now I want to ask you about the incident in your garden that you've also mentioned to officers?'

'It was Ian who found the flowers,' Mrs Stevenson answered, looking across to her husband.

'It wasn't really much to be honest," Mr Stevenson said. "I didn't think much of it at the time. I've only mentioned it because it was out of the ordinary.'

'Can you take me through it, Mr Stevenson?' Alix said.

'Well, as I say, it wasn't much. It happened about two weeks ago. It was the middle of the week, Wednesday or Thursday. It would have been about half ten at night. Our Hayles had not long got in. She'd been with some of her uni friends going through their essays or whatever. She grabbed some fruit from the bowl, said she'd see me tomorrow, that she was whacked, and went upstairs. I was locking up and turning off the telly, and then went through to the kitchen to make sure the back door was locked when I saw that the security light was on. I didn't think much about it because next door has a cat and it's triggered it a few times.

'Anyway, I looked out, saw everything was okay, turned out the lights and went to bed. The next morning, I got up for work and went down to the kitchen and was just filling up the kettle when I noticed some flowers lying in the middle of the garden. I thought at first they might be ours, dug up by the cat or maybe a fox and went outside, and they were just lying there. A bunch of wild flowers. Not from our garden. And they had a pink ribbon around them. I wondered if someone had thrown them over the fence, because there's a path at the bottom, and so I picked them up and binned them.' He shrugged his shoulders. 'That's it.'

Changing tack, Alix quizzed them about their daughter's lifestyle, in particular what they knew about her university life.

Rebecca was brought into the conversation with regards her relationship with her elder sister.

Hamlet wrote everything down. An hour later, happy she had exhausted their interview, Alix pushed herself up from the sofa and handed over her card with contact details, telling them she would be in touch, and made for the door. As she and Hamlet stepped into the hallway, Rebecca said, 'I don't know if this is worth mentioning but she received a wedding invitation.'

Alix locked on to Rebecca's concerned look. 'Wedding invitation?'

'Yeah. It came in the post a couple of weeks ago. It was in a pink envelope addressed to Hayles. I was just off to college and Hayles was still in bed. I thought it was a card at first and took it up to her. Made a joke about it being from that admirer of hers and she said "very funny," and I told her to open it, so she did. It was this wedding invitation with her name on it and in the date was written "soon" and in the venue it just said "surprise." She showed it to me and then tore it up.'

'A couple of weeks ago, you say?' said Alix.

Rebecca nodded.

'And Hayley had no idea who it was from?'

'No.'

'You said she tore it up. Do you know if it's still here?'

'It might still be in her bin in her bedroom. That's where she's likely to have thrown it. I went off to college so I didn't see what she did with it.'

Alix dragged her gaze away from Rebecca, switching it between Mr and Mrs Stevenson. 'Do you mind if we go up and have a look in Hayley's room?'

Mr Stevenson showed them upstairs. Four doors led off the landing, three were bedrooms and one was the bathroom. Hayley's room was the middle of the three bedrooms.

Alix and Hamlet slipped on latex gloves and went straight to a waste bin beside a dressing table. After a quick rummage among soiled make-up cleansing pads, receipts and a couple of pieces of cellophane packaging, Alix found the torn-up wedding invitation, together with a ripped pink envelope. She recovered them carefully, placing them in exhibit bags.

Hamlet and Alix searched the rest of Hayley's room. It would already have had a cursory examination by officers taking the initial report but they wanted to go through things again. The room had built-in wardrobes and a chest of drawers with a few shelves that held personal items on them, mainly books and CD's with a couple of framed school photos of Hayley in her early teens.

Hamlet watched as Alix tackled the wardrobe first and then went through the drawers, lifting and moving aside items to see if anything was tucked beneath or between. There was nothing. At the shelves she lifted off each book and CD, shaking the books upside down and opening up the CD cases to see if anything was inside. Again nothing.

Mr Stevenson remained in the doorway and Alix checked from time to time if he had noticed anything that shouldn't be there. Satisfied that the wedding invitation and its envelope were the only items that warranted scrutiny, Alix handed them to Hamlet and they made their way back downstairs, where Alix wound up their visit by telling the family that if they had any information, or wished to ask anything, they shouldn't hesitate to call her on the number on the card she had given them.

As Alix and Hamlet made their way back to the car, Alix said, 'Were you okay with all that, Hamlet?'

'That was interesting,' he answered.

'Any thoughts from what you've seen or heard?'

'I'm sure the phone calls, the flowers placed in the middle of the garden and the wedding invitation are linked.'

'Good. Me too.'

'You're probably on the same wavelength as to thinking this is a stalker?'

Alix returned a quick nod.

'Well, my experience of dealing with individuals who stalk is that they usually have some type of personality disorder. Generally an Obsessive Compulsive Disorder, or OCD for short. In the case of Hayley, my initial thoughts are that someone has built up some form of relationship with her, enough for it to be some form of obsession for him to pursue.'

'You think she might know them then?'

'Not necessarily, but she might well have had some passing dealings with the individual that has triggered something to make them believe that Hayley has an interest in them. If I was a betting man I would set my reputation on it being the latter individual. Someone who has a fixated fantasy about Hayley. Most people who have Obsessive Compulsive Personality Disorder alienate themselves from forming close social contact with anyone.'

'So, from what you're saying, she could have been abducted by someone who is fixated with her?'

'I fear that's a strong possibility, Alix. The invitation, the flowers. Those are usually things you send to someone you love or admire. From cases I've read, and from my experience of working with patients who have similar personality disorders, so long as she doesn't do anything to make him

31

think he hasn't any chance of forming a relationship with her then she isn't in any immediate danger.'

Alix popped the locks of the car and hurriedly climbed into the driver's seat. 'Let's just hope she has enough about her to keep him on her side. When we get back, you need to feed in your thoughts straight away.' She snapped on her seatbelt and fired up the engine.

FOUR

The large ground-floor room of the training centre, normally used for passing out parades of new recruits, had been set out for a press conference to seek publicity as to the whereabouts of Hayley Stevenson. It was the second day of the investigation and while the Major Investigation Team still had a lot of actions to work on, the Yorkshire-based press were inundating HQ Media Communication Team for information, already linking her disappearance to Jessica McKenna. Whilst the force wanted to play that down they knew they had to address it to save any future embarrassment and allay the worries of the McKenna family, who were relying upon the police to keep their daughter's name in the public domain in the hope of getting some news.

Lauren Simmerson was heading up the conference, supported by DCI Karl Jackson. Hamlet watched as Jackson scanned the audience of chatting journalists before him, tightening the knot of his tie into his buttoned collar. In his expensive charcoal suit, he looked more the consummate politician than a seasoned chief of detectives. To the left of them sat Mr and Mrs Stevenson, who displayed looks of bewilderment as they stared at the two rows of seated journalists and the three camera operators with accompanying sound crew at the back; SKY TV, BBC Look North and Yorkshire ITV were all represented plus the local media.

Lauren gave the Stevensons a comforting smile, and, getting back a nervous nod from them, she glanced at the opening lines of her prepared statement and cleared her throat noisily.

The room fell to a hush.

'Good morning, everyone,' she began. 'Thank you for attending this conference which has been called to gain the public's help in finding 21-year-old Hayley Stevenson who was last seen by friends just before midnight on Saturday, four days ago. The last known sighting of Hayley was on Northumberland Road in Sheffield, close to the university she attends. I am now going to hand you over to Mr Stevenson who wants to talk a bit about his daughter and ask you for your help.'

Lauren set down her papers and turned to Mr Stevenson. The idea to bring in the Stevensons had come from the media department, and although initially there had been reluctance on their part which had required some gentle persuasion by Alix, they had eventually agreed. In the drafting of the press statement Lauren had included Hamlet's thoughts that Hayley was being held captive by someone. For the present time it was decided to hold back on revealing the calls to her mobile, which would give them breathing space whilst the technical people examined her phone data. They were also not disclosing the anonymous wedding invitation posted to Hayley. There were many enquiries in the system to try and trace where that came from.

Hamlet would like to have been present but it only needed one journalist to recognise him and that would distract the sole purpose of the press conference. Instead, he was with Alix in the adjoining room, the other side of a dividing partition that had been left slightly ajar at one end so they could see and hear without being conspicuous.

Mr Stevenson's notes shook in his trembling hands. 'Hayley is our eldest daughter...' he began, his voice shaking. He went on to talk about how she had survived meningitis when she was eight and had wanted to be a nurse following her hospitalisation at the Children's Hospital, and how she had worked hard at school to achieve that, and was now attending the university where she was training to become a nurse, specialising in paediatrics. 'Hayley's disappearance is completely out of character. Even when she goes away for a few days or on holiday she rings us every day. Hayley is a good and kind person who just wants to help people. She wouldn't harm a fly. So, if anyone is holding her, we ask you not to harm her and we beg you to let her go. Her younger sister is missing her. We are missing her. Her whole family are missing her.' Mr Stevenson let out a heavy breath. Sweat rimmed his forehead. He looked drained.

Lauren took back the proceedings, thanking Mr Stevenson before turning to the reporters. 'I'll take questions now.' Hands instantly shot up. Lauren selected a young woman in the front row.

'Emma Price, *Yorkshire Post*. Is it right, Detective Inspector, that you have found Hayley's mobile and driving licence close to where she was last seen and that her phone was deliberately broken? Do you believe Hayley has come to some harm?'

There had been much speculation over social media since Hayley's disappearance, especially the finding of her damaged phone. Lauren answered calmly, 'I can confirm that Hayley's mobile and driving licence were found early on Sunday morning by a passer-by on Northumberland Road where Hayley was last seen. And I can confirm that her mobile was damaged but we are unsure how that came about. It was found to the side of the road so it could have been run over by a passing car. Can I please make it clear that at this time we are treating this case as an unexplained disappearance. And only that. There is nothing to suggest at this stage of our enquiries that Hayley has come to any harm.'

More hands shot up as Lauren finished. She selected a man in his forties on the second row.

'Martin Wise, *Calendar News*. Are you looking at the possibility that Hayley's disappearance could be linked with that of twenty-year-old Jessica McKenna who disappeared eighteen months ago?'

Lauren responded, 'We are keeping an open mind on that, Martin. Although at this stage we have nothing to suggest that the two are linked, we cannot ignore the fact that we have two young women of similar age, both from Sheffield, who have gone missing in mysterious circumstances. With regards to Jessica, her enquiry is still open and is being investigated separately until anything else suggests otherwise.'

Lauren picked out another raised hand. It belonged to a straw-haired young man at the end of the second row.

'Matt Ross, *Sheffield Telegraph*. I have two questions, Detective Inspector. Picking up on the last question, both Jessica and Hayley's disappearances have occurred late at night after they have been on a night out with friends. First, should we be worried that someone could be abducting young women from the streets of Sheffield? And second, can you confirm that Hayley Stevenson was working as an escort at a local strip club?'

The room turned into a pandemonium.

The entire MIT was in lockdown. Lauren had called everyone in and was standing at the front of the room, her face still a blush of embarrassment and anger after what should have been a straightforward press conference had erupted into a frenzy.

Lauren said through gritted teeth, 'Will someone please explain to me how that journalist just hijacked my press conference with this shit about Hayley Stevenson being an escort? Not only that, her parents had to hear that from the press. Why wasn't I given this information before? I've been made to look like I haven't got a clue what's happening with my investigation.'

'We didn't know,' said a hesitant voice and everyone's eyes centred on the spokesman. It was DC Nick Lewis, who was one of the most experienced on the team. 'We've only just found out from social media ourselves, boss.'

'Please tell me it's not true then.'

'It could be, boss,' he returned and after a short pause added, 'Apparently, the *Sheffield Telegraph* released a digital feature about Hayley's disappearance to promote the press conference. It resulted in a series of social media postings from several men who have said they've seen Hayley working as a pole dancer at the Pink Rhino lap-dancing club.'

Lauren sucked in a breath. 'Damn. This is going to change the whole complexity of this investigation. The focus will be everything we don't want it to be. I want this story bottomed and bottomed quickly. I want the manager of that club visited and spoken with, soon as. Until that's done, every enquiry, with the exception of viewing CCTV, is on hold. We brief here again at two o'clock and see what we've got. I hope to God that this journalist is just talking shit, but something tells me he isn't.'

FIVE

As Alix drove away from the complex with Hamlet in the passenger seat, it was starting to rain. What had started out as a lovely clear day was now dark and foreboding, storm clouds tumbling over the hills of Sheffield.

'Well, that didn't quite go to plan,' Hamlet said, his eyes glancing over the folder Lauren had handed him after the briefing.

'I feel sorry for the boss. How on earth the press got that before us, I don't know. Someone had to have tipped them off. My bet it was one of the guys who posted it on social media. If Lauren finds out who it is she'll have his bollocks.'

'That journalist is not going to give up his source though, is he? It was interesting to note what paper he worked for.'

'The *Sheffield Telegraph*?' Alix said with derision.

'Yes. Sister paper of *The Star*. I'm just thinking about the trouble you and I had with their crime correspondent, Kieran Croft. I can't help but think that it's a backlash because of what happened to him at my place.'

Alix shot him a sideways glance. 'Don't remind me about him. He got me suspended. I've always felt sympathy for the victim but with him I don't. He had it coming.'

'I lost my job and friends because of him. And I had to go into hiding because of the muck he wrote about me,' Hamlet responded solemnly. 'Remember how he targeted both of us after he found out where I lived and followed you there, hinting that you and I were having some kind of sexual relationship? It was him snooping around my place that got him killed. Trying to dish up dirt on us, not knowing that

Benson had sneaked into the cabin, waiting for me to come home. That newspaper caused us all kinds of problems, and they didn't offer one jot of an apology even when Benson was caught. If you ask me, this is just the type of story they've been waiting for to embarrass the team.'

Alix acknowledged Hamlet's comments with a gentle nod, her mouth tightening. Taking a deep breath, letting it out as a heavy sigh, she said, 'Anyway, enough about Kieran Croft. You've got a new career to focus on. And we've got an important task to do. What was the name of this manager we're meeting?'

Hamlet glanced down at the folder in his lap. 'Harry Malvern. I spoke to him earlier to arrange an interview.'

'Did he say much on the phone?'

'Only that he'd received several calls from reporters this morning about Hayley but he hasn't said anything to them because he hasn't yet managed to get hold of his personnel manager to confirm if she works there or not. They employ almost two dozen women as dancers, plus bar staff and waitresses, and most of the women go by a pseudonym to protect themselves from unwanted attention and it's their stage name he knows most of them by. He's looked on the internet and seen Hayley's photograph and thinks she looks familiar. He'll meet us at the club before twelve.'

Alix parked in the underground car park of Snig Hill police station and she and Hamlet made their way on foot across the city centre to the Pink Rhino, which was just beyond the City Hall. The entire frontage of the club was made up of smoked glass windows, several of them displaying its signature logo of a pink silhouette of a scantily clad woman in an erotic pose. They could just make out that lights were on through the smoked glass as they approached.

'Someone's here,' Alix said, making for the entrance door.

It was pulled open before she had time to grab the handle. In the gap appeared a six-foot-tall bearded man in his early forties wearing a Barbour jacket and jeans.

'Can I help you?' he asked sternly, his gaze swinging from Alix to Hamlet.

Alix showed her ID, quickly answering, 'DS Rainbow, DC Mottrell,' then asked, 'Harry Malvern?'

His firm look relaxed. 'Yes. Just making sure you weren't reporters.' He threw the door open further and stepped aside to let them in.

The club was laid out with black leather seating and wooden tables all warmly lit by low-wattage ceiling lighting. The floors were polished wood and a long black leather-fronted bar was set along one wall. On the far wall was its signature pink logo and beneath that the words 'Gentleman's private club'.

Hamlet took in the setting, trying to imagine what the place was like when operating. He had never been in a lap-dancing club before, only seen them on TV, and then they were usually portrayed as seedy strip joints. This place looked anything but, he thought, as his gaze swept around the plush room.

Harry Malvern locked the door and said, 'We can talk here or go up to my office. We don't open until four. I've come in early because of your phone call.'

'And it's very good of you, Mr Malvern,' said Alix. 'We appreciate that. We don't want to take up too much of your time, so we can talk down here.'

'Please, call me Harry,' he said, showing them to a semi-circular booth of black leather, a low-level wooden table in the centre. 'Can I get you both a drink? I've switched on the coffee machine.'

'A coffee would be lovely,' Alix returned, 'no sugar, just milk, thanks,' she added.

Hamlet nodded. 'Coffee's good, thank you. Milk and one sugar please.'

As Harry headed over to the bar, Alix watched the tall man stride across the floor. 'Put your eyes back in their sockets, Alix, and stop drooling,' Hamlet whispered.

Alix turned sharply, catching his grin. 'What are you on about? I was just keeping my eye on him. Detective work if you want to know.'

'Oh yes, I believe you; others wouldn't.'

She let out a light laugh and gave him a nudge. 'For that, Detective Mottrell, you can take notes and fill in the form.'

Harry returned with three coffees on a tray, set them down on the table, positioned a cup in front of Alix and Hamlet and slid into the booth, arranging his jacket as he settled back into the leather. 'You want to ask me about Hayley?'

Alix took out a picture of Hayley from her bag and showed it to him. 'Does she work here?'

'That's the same photo they're showing on the internet. And yes, I've not long found out she does work here.'

Alix put the photo back in her bag.

'When you rang me, I didn't know for sure, but since your call I've spoken with our personnel manager, Sharon, and she's confirmed she's on our books. We took her on as a dancer just over six months ago now, and I'm told she generally works Fridays and Saturdays. She covers 8 p.m. until midnight on both nights. She has occasionally done Sunday afternoons if one of the regular women hasn't been able to make it. The Saturday that's just gone, which I understand is when she went missing, she'd arranged with Sharon to work 4 p.m. until 8 p.m. She'd got other arrangements apparently that she needed to get to afterwards.'

Alix gave him an understanding nod. She knew from Hayley's friends that they had arranged to meet up at Bar One at 9 o'clock that night and she was there on time.

Harry set down his cup. 'We have CCTV. It's on a seven-day loop so we'll still have Saturday's on record. It covers the area down here, except the toilets. It doesn't cover upstairs where the girls get changed, I'm afraid, but you'll be able to see Hayley all the time she was dancing on the podium. The girls on the pole tend to do half an hour on and half an hour off. Oh, and by the way, at the club Hayley was known as Poppy. I believe I mentioned on the phone that all the girls have a pseudonym here to try and protect their identity. I didn't know her that well I'm afraid. I only know a couple of the girls well enough to chat with because Sharon looks after them. That's her job. Mine is to look after our clients and their guests.' Light-heartedly he added, 'Make sure they spend lots of money.'

'So, you didn't know Hayley well at all then?' asked Alix.

'Not really, I'm afraid. Just enough to say hello to when she came in and ask if she was all right if I saw her taking her break, because, as I said, Sharon looks after the girls. She arranges their schedule, hours of work and pays them. I look after our members, the VIP's and guests.'

'Would you happen to know if Hayley had any problems with any of the members or guests?' Alix asked.

'Nothing comes to mind. I can ask Sharon. You can appreciate some of our clients do get carried away from time to time, but we have good door staff and security floating around to keep our girls safe. The girls who usually get the hassle from our customers are the ones who do the lap-dancing. Some of the punters get wandering hands and it requires security to intervene. We usually find a quiet word sorts them out.' He gave a wide smile. 'Some of our security scare me and I know them.'

'But Hayley never lap-danced?' Alix questioned.

'No. Some of the girls do both to earn extra money. Hayley just pole-danced.'

'Did you know Hayley was a student?'

'Not until the reporters told me. We never ask any of the girls what they do outside of the club. Many of the girls we employ do this job for extra income. I know that a couple of them are single mums, and that one of them is a nurse and two are teachers. Sharon has told me we have a few girls who are students but what they do outside this club doesn't interest me. All I'm interested in when they are here is that they do what they are paid to do and our clients have a good time.'

'Do any of your clients give you any cause for concern regarding their treatment of the women? Any of them ever complained to you about threats or intimidation?'

'None come to mind. As I say, much of the hassle the girls get is spontaneous from those who've had too much to drink and it's nipped in the bud straight away.' Harry finished his coffee and set down his cup. 'Look, I do my best to run this club as strictly to the licence conditions as possible. You may think I'm just saying this to satisfy you but it's the truth. You probably saw on the local news a few months ago we had a group of women outside here demonstrating, accusing us of exploiting the girls and challenging the renewal of our licence, and now we are regularly checked to see we don't breach anything.

'This is not a strip-club, as some would think. We look after our girls. We do our best to protect them. We don't encourage any of them to engage with clients other than lap-dance and we do everything possible to deter the use of drugs on the premises. We have some good clients who spend a lot of money here who do not want to draw attention to themselves and so we also want to protect them as well. I can put my hand on my heart when I say we do our damnedest to keep to the letter of the law as possible.

'Since I found out this morning about Hayley going missing, I've spoken with Sharon about whether she was involved with any of our known clients and she tells me that as far as she's aware, she wasn't. Sharon is willing to speak with you if it's of any help, but I think she'll only be able to tell you what I have already said. If Hayley was on the game, as those reporters who've rang me have said, all I can say is that she was wasn't carrying on her activities in this club. And as for CCTV, I'll have Saturday's footage copied as soon as Gerry, our security man, comes in.'

On the way home that evening Hamlet called in at the supermarket. Wherever possible he tried to cook fresh food but he had a feeling that he would be working long hours until his next day off and so he stocked up with microwave meals-for-one for the week.

As a last-minute thought he grabbed a copy of that evenings edition of the *Sheffield Telegraph* to see what they had made of that morning's conference. The headline shouted **MISSING WOMAN IN SEX INDUSTRY**.

It was just what the murder team didn't want. Hayley's sex life would now be the feature of the tabloid stories rather than the matter of her disappearance and that could completely throw their enquiries.

That afternoon's briefing had almost been a council of war against the press, with Lauren hitting home that no one must speak to any journalist, and from here on every press release would be carefully constructed to divert the sex angle involving Hayley.

It wasn't going to be easy. The press loved scandal. And though in this case it was information that was damaging for the enquiry, the information they had been given about Hayley Stevenson's life outside of university and away from home had been useful. It provided Hamlet with a clear point of focus with the investigation.

He recalled the conversation he'd had with Alix about victimology and that was now at the forefront of his thoughts. He was strongly of the opinion that Hayley's part-time job had something to do with the disturbing phone calls she had received. And more than likely the anonymous wedding invitation she had been sent and the flowers on the lawn. If that was the case, he had no doubt she had been stalked and more than likely abducted by the same person.

Two questions were now playing around in his head; did she know her abductor and why did he choose her among the others who worked at the club? He hadn't raised this in the briefing because it was only his second day on the job, but he knew sooner rather than later that he should. It was something they had to look at. And they also needed to now look and see if Jessica McKenna had also been a dancer, which might answer questions about her unexplained disappearance. He would run it past Alix tomorrow before he put it to the briefing.

SIX

The next morning in MIT, Lauren called out 'Developments everyone,' bringing the room to silence. She continued, 'Just before six thirty last night the Stevensons received a phone call from an unknown male who said that he had Hayley and indicated she was safe. He also said words to the effect that she had cheated on him but as long as she behaves she won't be harmed.

'Mr Stevenson instantly contacted the family liaison officer, who ran a check on the caller's number and found it to be an unregistered pay-as-you-go mobile number that had since been disconnected.

'DC West then contacted me and we spent several hours last night with Mr and Mrs Stevenson going back over the call, trying to determine if it was anyone they know. Mrs Stevenson took the call, and said the caller was male, but she did not recognise his voice.

'What is of concern is that at no time during the call was there any ransom demand or an indication that Hayley would be freed. We have now put a recording device on the line in case there are any further calls. I have actioned the tracing of the phone but it's my guess it's probably been bought off eBay or one of the marketplace sites online, so it'll be untraceable.

'I have another important matter to tell you in relation to the number used by the caller but I just want to hold on to that for a moment because I want to keep the focus on last night's call to the Stevensons.' Looking at Hamlet, she said, 'I know I'm putting you on the spot here, Hamlet, but can you give us any thoughts about what I've just said?

'The enquiries we have made so far don't reveal Hayley being in any relationship with anyone at the present time. We know of two boyfriends she had before she went to university and they have already been checked out by officers. One has not been in contact with her since they split up four years ago, and the other from a relationship when she was fifteen follows her on social media. Both of those relationships simply fizzled out. There was nothing acrimonious between them. As far as we know, Hayley was not promiscuous. Her lap-dancing work appears to be merely that — work.' She paused again, this time giving Hamlet a look that begged a response.

For a few seconds Hamlet composed his thoughts, then he responded with a gentle steady tone — the way he used to address his audience at clinician's meetings. It had been a long time since someone had asked him for his professional opinion. 'The more you look into the manner of Hayley's disappearance, and the circumstances prior to that, the more convinced I am that the person who has Hayley has Obsessive Compulsive Personality Disorder in some form.

'When Obsessive Compulsive Disorder coincides with another personality disorder, then it can result in patterns of behaviour that most people would regard as unpredictable and disturbing. It could lead to psychosis with the person believing in things that don't exist. We generally see this in cases where a fan becomes obsessed with a celebrity, believing that they are the answer to their dreams and so begin stalking them.

'In the case of Hayley, I believe we are looking at something similar. For some reason the abductor has become obsessed with her and it's my guess he will have been stalking her for some time. The flowers and wedding invitation are his way of connecting with her and relieving the stress of his obsession with her.

'However, discovering that she dances at the Pink Rhino does not fit with the idealistic impression he has created of her in his mind. He has put her on a pedestal. Like the celebrity obsession, Hayley is the answer to his dreams and so to discover that she performs before all those leering men forms the belief she has cheated on him and he needs to take her away from that environment. In a way, he may feel he is protecting her.

'Now that he has her, he will be going through the dilemma of what to do next. The comment he made to Mrs Stevenson about her remaining unharmed so long as she behaves is his way of addressing how he is dealing with the problem.'

'Do you think it's someone Hayley knows, and if so, would he harm her?'

The questions came from a man three seats along. Hamlet thought his first name was Ben, but as with the other members of the squad he hadn't had time to get to know him yet.

Hamlet responded, 'I rather think it's someone she doesn't know, but I could be wrong. It could be someone she may only have met briefly. Someone she's chatted to in the pub, for instance. Hayley is an attractive young woman and everyone we've talked to so far say she is a lovely person. You usually find that individuals with this condition tend to be shy and deliberately isolate themselves from forming relationships, so he won't have asked her out or anything like that, but she just might have made some connection with him that's triggered a fascination for her. Hence the stalking. Would he harm her? Possibly, if Hayley doesn't behave like he wants her to.'

A hush fell around the room and people exchanged concerned looks with one another.

'Thank you for your input, Hamlet,' said Lauren. 'You have left us with no illusions on how important it is that we do everything possible to find out where Hayley is. And quickly.'

'Just another thing, boss,' Hamlet interjected. 'It is more than likely that Hayley is not the first person he has been fixated on in this way.'

A few heads jerked his way, including Alix's.

'It's funny you should say that, Hamlet,' Lauren returned, 'because, as I mentioned earlier, one of the other developments is the fact that the number that Mrs Stevenson was called from yesterday evening is among one of those that is listed in Hayley's mobile phone log which she blocked because of the crank calls. She received three calls from the number, the first of which was two months ago. And I have learned this morning from the analyst who checked Jessica McKenna's mobile phone data that she also received two calls from this same number prior to her disappearance eighteen months ago.' Lauren straightened and pursed her lips 'After what Hamlet has just said, and the information I have just given you, it would be fair to state that our investigation has just cranked up a notch.'

Alix turned into the park-and-ride car park at Sheffield's Valley Centertainment Leisure Park and cruised past the sparse lines of parked vehicles looking for Hamlet's Range Rover. She spotted it in the top row, parked facing the tram lines, and pulled into an empty space two slots away. She climbed into Hamlet's car.

'Tell me why at ten at night you find it so important to drag me out of a nice warm bath to meet you in a car park in an entertainment centre that closes in a couple of hours?'

Hamlet turned to face Alix, his mouth breaking into a grin. He had been sat here for half an hour, thinking through the evening's planned foray. 'I thought I might interest you in some nocturnal detective work.'

'The last time you involved me in nocturnal detective work, we ended up at a derelict children's home with James Harry Benson and me saving your sorry arse, if I recall.'

Hamlet let out a hearty laugh. 'It's nothing as exciting as that I'm afraid.'

'So, enlighten me, why you dragged me here?'

Hamlet picked a paper file from off the back seat and dropped it into Alix's lap. 'I took Jessica McKenna's file home with me and went through it again while I was having something to eat. I've gone through all the statements from the friends who last saw her and it was here where she spent her last hours before she disappeared. I wanted to familiarise myself with the area where she was last seen and take the last journey she made before she disappeared. I thought you might be interested.'

Alix opened up the file. The first page she saw was the missing person report with a photograph of Jessica fastened top-left. It was the same image that now featured with her profile details on the incident board back in MIT.

'When you say 'take the last journey', you mean on the tram?'

'That's the idea. I want to catch one at the same time as the one she took. And although it's not the same time of year, I want to get a feel for what she might have seen and heard, especially what it was like at this time of night when she got off at Cricket Inn Road to make her way home. Are you up for that?'

Alix shrugged her shoulders. 'I don't know what we'll learn, but I'll give it a shot. Especially now you've dragged me out all this way.'

'Good.' Hamlet took Jessica's missing file back from Alix and climbed out of the car. Alix followed, slinging her bag over her shoulder.

They set off across the car park, heading for the steps that took them to the tram-stop less than a hundred metres away.

Hamlet said, 'I'm guessing this place would have been very much like this even eighteen months ago in November. It's a very popular place. The concert arena is only a stone's throw away and the cinema and eating places are all next to one another. I had a look around before you got here and the cinema especially is bustling. I've been watching people come and go and the majority of people who visit here use their cars. The trams are very quiet. And according to the statements, that's how Jessica and her friends arrived and left on the night she disappeared.

'The two friends Jessica came with that Saturday evening got on at Hyde Park where they live in the flats, and joined Jessica, who was already on the tram. They travelled to the cinema, where they watched a movie, and then went to Frankie & Benny's for a bite to eat and something to drink and then caught the 10.25 tram from here back home.' He skipped up the steps. 'Come on, we're just in time to catch the same one.'

Alix caught up with him and followed him across the tracks to the stop. 'You've certainly done your research, Hamlet,' she said, taking her warrant ID card out from her bag to claim her free travel.

Standing beneath the shelter, Hamlet said, 'It's a very thorough file. Very detailed. I've learned a lot about Jessica. Like Hayley, she was a student at Sheffield University. She was studying to be a primary school teacher. The two friends she was with that night were on the same course but they didn't know one another before uni.

'Jessica was heterosexual but not in a current relationship, though she had a number of close friends who were males. Two of those joined them at the cinema that night — they'd come earlier for a drink, and they got on the tram to go back with them, staying on after the women had all got off until they reached the university stop, where they were in digs nearby.

'Those young men were alibied by CCTV and witnesses. They all made mention in their statements of Jessica telling them about several nuisance calls she had received from a man and that, like Hayley, she too had blocked two numbers, and that she thought someone was stalking her although she hadn't seen anyone.' Hamlet stopped talking briefly as he spotted the yellow Supertram trundling toward them. 'We now know that those calls came from unregistered mobiles and that two calls were the same number found on Hayley Stevenson's phone.'

'I'm impressed,' Alix said, as the tram came to a halt.

The doors hissed open and they climbed aboard. It was relatively empty and they took a double seat close to the door, Alix showing her warrant card to the conductor as she sat down.

Cricket Inn Road was five stops along and it took them just over five minutes to get there. Two other passengers got off with them and Hamlet and Alix held back to let them pass, watching them walk away. The tram stop was in a natural dip and for a moment Alix and Hamlet looked around and listened. Except for the sound of cars passing on the road above them there was no other noise. The area was well lit, warm orange light pouring from the overhead lamps, and Alix watched Hamlet set his gaze on the opposite stop.

'What are you looking for?' Alix asked.

Hamlet moved his gaze along the platform where it led to the footpath. 'Jessica was the first to get off the tram. Her two friends got off at the next stop and the two lads then carried on to the university stop. I'm just trying to get a feel for what it might have been like for Jessica when she got off at this time eighteen months ago. I thought it might have been busier than this, it being Saturday.'

'This part of Wybourn is quiet. This is the shopping and business area. The housing estate she lived in, which is across the main road, will be a lot busier.'

Hamlet set off walking, and Alix hurried after him. The slight incline took them up to the main road and here again Hamlet came to a stop. Alix almost bumped into him.

'Will you stop doing that, Hamlet!' she chuntered.

Hamlet smiled. 'Sorry. I'll warn you next time.' He scoured their location. 'If I was a young woman out at this time of night, on my own, I would keep to this side of the road, away from the pub, until I'd come to where I needed to cross over to the street where I lived. The street lighting is good on this side, so any passing cars would be able to see me.'

'I like your thinking, doc,' Alix replied, tucking in beside him.

They neared a row of three shops, beyond which was a car park surrounded by a low wall. There was only one car parked in there, and it was empty. As they got to the door of the last shop Alix noticed a narrow opening between the end of the shop and the start of the car park. Hamlet came to a stop by the entrance. He was standing at the beginning of a thin alleyway that ran the length of the building. The back half of the alleyway was in darkness.

'Now this is interesting,' murmured Hamlet, stepping into the passage.

'On to something?' Alix asked, coming up close.

'Don't know,' he responded, edging slowly along.

There was a lot of rubble around and it was getting gloomier the further they crept along, the building shielding most of the streetlight.

Halfway along Hamlet stopped, turning to look at Alix. 'We know Jessica got off the tram here because her friends saw her, and CCTV at the tram stop captured her walking in this direction, but after that there are no other sightings. We also know that Jessica had several anonymous phone calls in the weeks leading up to her disappearance and also she told friends she thought she was being followed...'

Alix nodded. 'Yes.'

'Well, let's run with the scenario that whoever took Jessica was stalking her. It wouldn't take them too long to learn her habits. She spent most of her days at uni, did most of her shopping at Meadowhall, sometimes meeting up with friends there, and her Friday and Saturday nights were usually spent with friends at Centertainment, either at the cinema or having a few drinks and something to eat.

'Although she had access to her parent's car she travelled nearly everywhere on the tram. A, because it was so convenient, and, B, because she got cheap travel with her student card. So, it wouldn't have been too hard to follow her and get to know her routine. And it would be my guess he will have been doing this for some time.

'A link's been made between Jessica and Hayley through the same unregistered phone number so if it's the same guy who's involved in Hayley's disappearance, my view is that he'll have been planning this moment for some time.

'Eighteen months ago, he'll have known that on a typical Saturday evening Jessica would be going to Centertainment to meet up with her friends, and know that she got off at this stop on her way back home and would be on her own at roughly this time. Knowing what her regular time back was, it wouldn't be too hard for him to follow her to Centertainment and hang around a while to make sure her plans weren't changed, and then set off back on the tram just before her and wait up somewhere until she walked past on her way home.

'Jessica goes up that street there,' he said, pointing opposite, where the road rose up a slight gradient into the estate. 'If I wanted to grab her, this is where I would lay up. Tucked back in here against the wall, maybe crouched down, so no one could see me, and I would wait for her to pass and then make my move.' He stabbed a finger at the car park next to them. 'I'm guessing our man would have a vehicle of some sort to carry her away in, given that she was not picked up on CCTV along here or anywhere nearby, and what better place to leave it ready, in the shadow of these shops, maybe with a door open, or the boot up.'

'Crikey, Hamlet, I think you could be on to something here.'

He delved into his pocket and brought out a small torch, switching it on. The powerful beam lit up their surroundings and he swept it around, keeping the light low to the floor. Taking one step at a time, slowly arcing the beam around, he swept the lower part of the building to his left, drifting the torch before him before swinging it towards the car park wall to his right. Six steps in, only a few yards from the metal gate, he stopped. 'What's that?' he exclaimed. The torchlight settled on something shiny.

Alix moved in beside him and picked it up, holding it in front of the beam. It was a small key with a yellow plastic fob. There were three numbers on the fob. Alix read them out. 'Two, one, four. It looks like a locker key.' She squatted down close to the building wall. 'Just hold your torch here will you, Hamlet?'

He settled the beam on the brickwork, holding it steady.

Alix suddenly exclaimed, 'Look at this,' and bending down further, circled her fingers around an area of staining on the brickwork close to the ground. 'Is that what I think it is?'

It was well after 2 a.m. before Hamlet got home and the first thing he did was let Lucky out for a toilet break and give him some food. He felt guilty for neglecting the little terrier and spent the best part of half an hour making a fuss of him before getting himself a sandwich and beer. He especially needed a beer.

He was hyped up. After discovering the locker key and suspicious staining on the wall, Alix had instantly phoned the DI. Lauren had turned out and while she hadn't been too impressed with their gung-ho exploits without informing her, she had recognised the importance of the find and had the location immediately sealed off and a uniformed officer put in situ to protect the scene for the following morning.

As he plonked himself down on the sofa and took the head off his beer, Hamlet knew he wasn't going to be able to get to sleep that night.

SEVEN

Shortly before 8 a.m. the next morning, Hamlet and Alix arrived in an unmarked car into the car park next to the row of shops at Wybourn where they had been the night before. Blue and white tape was strung across the entrance to the narrow alleyway and a uniformed officer was standing guard. Lauren was already there, sat in her car, and she got out to greet them.

'I've just spoken with the CSI supervisor. He's coming over personally to handle this. He should be with us before nine.'

'What do you want us to do?' Alix asked.

'I can already see some members of the public are out wondering what's going on,' Lauren said, dipping her head in the direction of a couple of people using their mobiles to either video or take photos of them. 'If this area is the site of Jessica's disappearance, I'd hate her parents to find out from either the press or social media, so will you give them a call to inform them we're following up on some information we've received but we haven't got anything concrete to tell them at this time? Also, check if Jessica owns a locker key the same as the one you've found.'

Alix nodded. 'Anything else, boss?'

Lauren shook her head. 'Not for now. I'm going to get back and give the team an update. You look after the scene and liaise with CSI. If you get anything give me a call.' She pulled her car keys from her coat pocket. 'And I know I gave you both a bit of a bollocking last night, which you deserved by the way, but I want to say good work you two. I'm keeping my fingers crossed this could be something significant.'

Alix thanked her, watched her get into her vehicle, then she retrieved Jessica McKenna's file from their vehicle and leafed through it until she came to the information she wanted. She dialled the number listed on the form.

After a couple of rings it was answered by Jessica's mother, and while she expanded on what Lauren told her to say, Alix was conscious that she didn't want to either upset or build up the woman's hopes with regards to their discovery, so kept the conversation informative but not revealing. When she mentioned the locker key, she hit the jackpot.

'That smile tells me you have news,' Hamlet said.

She caught his gaze. 'I've just learned Jessica was a member of the gym at Ponds Forge, and on the afternoon of the day she disappeared she went there for a swim before she went out. Her mum's just said that Jessica rang her around teatime to say she'd decided to do an extra class there, and was going to grab a snack, and then go out from there to meet up with her mates. She didn't come home. That bit wasn't in her statement.'

'So the locker key belongs to the gym?'

'We'll soon find out. As soon as CSI get here, we'll have a run down.'

It was shortly after nine when CSI arrived. Alix briefed the two forensic officers as to what she and Hamlet had discovered, pointing to the low wall where she had found the locker key and indicating the stains on the brickwork, where, in the daylight, she now noticed that the splashes were far more evident. Then, while the two officers got themselves suited up, she told them that she and Hamlet had a quick job to do, would be back within the hour, and then jumped into their car and drove off to the city.

At Ponds Forge Alix made themselves known at reception and asked to speak to the manager. The manager instantly confirmed the key was one of theirs and took them downstairs to where the locker area was located. As they made their way towards the gymnasium section Alix picked out where the CCTV cameras were, noting how well the sports centre was covered and cursing that any footage of Jessica was long gone, such was the time that had elapsed from her last visit.

Coming to a halt at locker 214, Alix put on a pair of latex gloves, fished out the key from the evidence bag and inserted it into the lock. The door clicked open with a quarter turn and Alix opened it wider so they could get a look.

Inside was a pink sports bag. Alix lifted it out, set it down on the floor and unzipped it. A stale sweaty smell greeted her as she began lifting out the contents: a towel, followed by a pair of trainers and then a pair of leggings. She gently laid them on the floor.

As she dipped her hand in again, she suddenly let out a soft 'hmm' and brought out a pink envelope, the flap of which was open. She glanced quickly up at Hamlet, giving him an excited look, and with a finger and thumb delicately slipped out a single piece of paper. It was a wedding invitation. Jessica's name was written on it with the words "soon" scribed in the date section and "surprise" in the venue.

'Exactly the same as Hayley's,' said Hamlet. 'It definitely looks like the same person has taken both Jessica and Hayley.'

Alix motored back to Wybourn, getting Hamlet to update Lauren on their discovery; checks now needed to be made of other incidents or attacks reported around the area where Jessica had been snatched. They also needed to pull up the details of any sex offenders who lived, or had been living, in the locality eighteen months ago. It was standard procedure now they were confident the alleyway was where Jessica had been abducted.

They made their way across to the two CSI officers, where they were given news — the reagent had detected the stains to be blood and swabs had been taken for DNA testing. It would be the best part of a week before the results came back. Alix thanked the officers and told them their job wasn't done yet, requesting they extended their search parameters.

Watching the officers returning to the alley, Alix turned to Hamlet. 'We'd have never found this if it hadn't been for you,' she said. 'Aren't you glad now that you joined the police? You'd have been wasted in your old job.'

'It's my old job that gave me this skill-set.'

'Well, the police need you much more than the NHS,' she added, giving him a gentle nudge. 'But don't let that go to your head, it's swelling up enough as it is.'

He let out a short laugh.

'Any further thoughts now we know this is more than likely the place where Jessica was taken?' Alix asked, returning her gaze to the two CSI's kickstarting their examination of the narrow passage again.

'Well, it certainly reaffirms my initial thoughts about how Jessica's attacker has gone about his preparation before he's carried out his plan. Now I've seen this area it would be my guess that he's more than likely rehearsed this, not once, but several times before he's made his move. He'll have been here on multiple occasions, seeing what the area was like at night, until he was confident he could make his move with the minimum of risk of getting caught.

'The same with Hayley. The wedding invitations are proof we're looking for the same person. This is someone who creates a fantasy world around someone, who probably fashions various scenarios of being with them, and then sets out their stall to achieve that. And that would include following them around, watching most of their moves and firing up their imagination to build it up into reality. The abduction is the final step to achieving that reality.'

'I told you, you were wasted in your old job.'

'Maybe so. And holding on to what I've just said about Jessica and Hayley, you might not like what I'm going to say next.'

Alix threw him a puzzled look. 'What's that?'

'It's my guess Jessica wasn't his first. As I've said, a lot of work will have gone into making sure he wasn't going to be caught taking her. I think we should be looking at others he may have abducted, or at least stalked, prior to her.'

Alix's mouth set tight. 'Do you think Jessica is still alive?'

'Sadly, I think not. Especially with Hayley's abduction. It's my guess Hayley is her replacement.'

'Shit! So it's imperative we find Hayley. And soon.'

'We have to hope she has enough about her to keep him attracted to her,' he responded grimly.

CSI finished their examination of the scene just after 11 a.m., and after checking that they had collected everything of forensic value Alix thanked them and then let the shopkeepers know they could have access once more to the alleyway. Before leaving she ripped away the crime scene tape, took several photographs of the surroundings on her phone and let Lauren know she and Hamlet were on their way back to the office.

On arrival they grabbed a sandwich from the canteen and made their way up to the office. Lauren was there, writing up the latest material on Jessica McKenna's board.

Upon spotting them she made a beeline for them before they had reached their desks. 'There's a full briefing in ten minutes. I'll need your input so grab a drink and get settled,' she said.

Alix unwrapped her ham salad sandwich, took a few bites from it, and while chewing made herself and Hamlet a coffee. She had just managed to swallow the last mouthful of her lunch as Lauren brought the room to order and began the briefing.

'Everyone in this room has heard about the dramatic turn of events this investigation has taken over the last twelve hours,' Lauren began. 'Whilst Jessica McKenna's disappearance was brought to our attention following the disappearance of Hayley Stevenson, it had only been supposition that the two are linked. All that has now changed.

'Thanks to Alix and Hamlet, we are almost certain we know the location where Jessica was taken.' She zeroed in on Hamlet. 'I know I'm putting you on the spot again, Hamlet, and conscious that you have only just joined our team and aren't quite up to speed with the way we operate yet, but you're no stranger to giving talks like this. Can you go through last night's events and what you and Alix discovered this morning?'

Surprisingly, Hamlet felt his stomach lurch and he had to clear his throat twice before he started, but once he got going he found his confidence, and after giving a brief explanation about his thought processes that took him to Valley Centertainment, he gave a detailed account of his and Alix's movements leading up to the discovery in the alleyway.

At this point Alix came in and led the team through their visit to Ponds Forge sports centre that morning, describing what they had found in the locker. Alix held up the wedding invitation. 'This is identical to the one we found torn-up in Hayley's waste bin in her bedroom.'

'So, there we have it,' interjected Lauren. 'I think we can safely say we are looking for someone who has now abducted two young women. Hamlet has already told us his thoughts on the type of personality disorder our individual has, so you don't need me to tell you all the danger our man poses to young women out there until we catch him. It's imperative that that moment comes sooner than later.

'In the meantime, we have the press to deal with. They have already put two and two together following CSI's activity at Wybourn. The communications department have been fending off calls all morning from them, and I've already had Jessica's and Hayley's parents on the phone, asking if it's true that the same person has taken their daughters, as the press have hinted to them. I've released the usual statement that it's an ongoing investigation and at this stage we can't comment, but the media aren't buying it. What we don't want is the young women of Sheffield panicking. And we need to make sure the wedding invitation information isn't leaked at this stage.'

'The Wedding Killer,' a man's voice called across the office.

All eyes turned on DC Nate Fox.

'What did you say, Nate?'' Lauren asked.

'The Wedding Killer, boss. That's who our guy is according to what Hamlet said about Jessica McKenna probably being dead, and the invites he's sending them.'

Lauren rolled her eyes. 'There's always someone who has to create a nickname. And how did I know it would be you, Nate?' she replied.

EIGHT

While Alix dealt with the admin side of the last twelve hours — chronicling the timeline, highlighting the evidential finds, writing them into her journal — Hamlet got to work searching through the national database of missing persons.

Following the briefing, he had asked Alix if he could run a search for other missing young women. 'What you usually find is that serial offenders make mistakes early on from which they perfect their act. I'm confident our man will have targeted others a long time before Jessica, and that is how we are going to find him,' he had said.

What he hadn't anticipated when he started the task was just how many police systems there were that held the information he required. There were two systems that had records of individuals who had harassed victims with nuisance phone calls, stalking and even breaking into their homes to steal items. Another system held data on offenders who had carried out all manner of sexual offences. And to cap it all, there were intelligence networks that collated information about individuals who were suspected of criminal behaviour. After learning all that, he quickly realised that he had a pretty daunting trial ahead and started his task by visiting The National Missing Persons Index to see where that took him.

An hour into his search he pushed aside the computer mouse, blowing out a frustrated 'Harrumph' noise.

'What's the matter, Hamlet?' Alix asked, looking up from her screen.

'This is going to take an eternity. I've put what details I can into the search parameters and it's throwing up hundreds of names. Isn't there an easy way?'

Alix issued a cynical grin. 'That is the easy way. I'm afraid that unless you have a name or partial name, date of birth, address even, then you are at the mercy of algorithms of the system. The lesson for today is that no matter how good the computer programmes are it's still the old-fashioned legwork and dogged determination of the detective that leads to us apprehending the villain.'

'I think we should release the information about the wedding invitations. That would cut the size of the task significantly.'

Alix's mouth set tight. 'I can see where you're coming from but that's not something we do. We hold on to information like that until we get our man. Then we know whether we've got the right person or not when they reveal it in interview.'

'But we could be searching forever and a day. Can't we circulate something internal with a warning not to release to the press? The sending of the invitations is our man's signature. Officers could well have dealt with a missing person where they have come across one and not realised the significance of it.'

Alix thought for a moment and then said, 'We'll run it past the boss. She may come up with a way we can do this without releasing the crucial evidence. In the meantime, plough on and see what you can come up with. Start with Sheffield missing persons first and work outwards.'

By the end of the day, by solely focussing on Sheffield, Hamlet had printed off the details of a dozen twenty-something women who had gone missing over the last four years and were still listed on the system as not returned. He highlighted the names of the officers who had completed the paperwork and created a file for each, stacking them in date order. He calculated it would take a couple of day's work to determine if they fitted into a pattern similar to Hayley and Jessica's disappearance.

Alix's head popped up above the desk divider. 'Fancy a drink after work?' she asked.

'Under normal circumstances I would jump at the offer, Alix, but Lucky's not been out since half six this morning.' Before she had time to reply, he added, 'Tell you what, why not come to mine? I've got some beers and wine in. We can walk Lucky and then I'll rustle us up some food.'

Closing down her computer, she replied, 'That sounds like a great idea, Hamlet. It'll be nice to have someone cook for me. And not to be eating alone for once.'

It was still daylight when Hamlet and Alix pulled into the clearing in front of the cabin, though only just. Another half hour and the day would give way to dusk.

Hamlet hopped up the steps onto the veranda and, pulling open the French doors, he was instantly greeted by Lucky, tail spiralling furiously. He bent down to ruffle his fur and then stepped into the lounge. Alix followed him in.

Tossing his car keys onto the coffee table he slipped off his suit jacket, threw it over the back of the sofa and headed back outside. 'I'll just do twenty minutes with him, let him run some energy off and then we'll have some food, eh?'

Alix nodded.

'Look, why don't you decide what you want to eat, and grab a glass of wine? Those flats of yours could get a bit messy in the woods,' he added, dipping his head toward her shoes. 'The same goes for your slacks. I can whiz him round in no time. What do you say?'

'I think that might be a good idea. Do you want me to start cooking?'

'No. I made the offer. This is my treat. You grab a glass of wine and just chill.' With that, he slipped off his brogues and put on a pair of walking boots by the door, and quick-stepped out of the cabin.

While he was gone, Alix removed the two bags of shopping from Hamlet's Range Rover that he had stopped to pick up on the way home, took them through to the kitchen, and, seeking out the white wine in the fridge, poured herself a glass and began unpacking. She saw he'd bought salad and some fruit and she washed it for him and left it on the side. He had bought two sirloin steaks and she put those to the back of the worktop out of the reach of Lucky.

She cracked open the window to let in some fresh air, and then made her way back into the lounge. She drifted over to the open French doors to see if there was any sign of Hamlet and Lucky, and, not seeing or hearing any sound of them she turned back to the room, where she noticed that the door to his study was ajar.

Hamlet had told her that his grandfather had a master craftsman build it. Without doubt it was a classic showpiece. Probably the best room in the cabin. She knew that Hamlet spent a lot of time in there, either reading some of the many hundreds of books that lined the shelves, or researching on his laptop.

She decided to have a nosy to see if he was up to anything new since becoming a detective. The moment she pushed open the door she saw a large pinboard on the opposite wall covered in all manner of newspaper cuttings and photographs. It was his own mini incident board capturing the sequence of murders James Harry Benson had committed.

She stepped forward, quickly scanning the contents. On there were all the local and national headlines recalling the atrocities he had carried out. Benson's murderous activities had started at the age of ten when he had killed his and Hamlet's parents, making it look like their bullying father had murdered their mother and then committed suicide. Then, at the age of fifteen he had killed a girlfriend in a fit of rage and buried her in a plot in a local cemetery. Her body had only been discovered nine months ago after Benson had come under the spotlight again. He had attacked and killed the doctor and his wife who had adopted Hamlet, before travelling across Sheffield where he had entered Hamlet's home and brutally killed his pregnant wife, Helen, leaving Hamlet with his arm and wrists slashed.

It had been those last acts that had seen Hamlet initially charged with his wife's and adoptive parents murders and placed in prison, though thanks to the work of his defence council he had managed to get released.

Nine months ago, Alix had taken a call from Hamlet informing her that he believed he had evidence that would prove he was innocent of murder and that James Herry Benson was responsible. She had taken some convincing, but the culmination of their work together had uncovered the truth. Benson had killed them all. Now he was in Broadmoor, his murderous spree making him one of Britain's most notorious serial killers.

'Spying on me?'

Alix spun around. Hamlet and Lucky were standing in the doorway. She hadn't heard them come in. 'I was just having a nosy. I can see you've kept it updated.'

He nodded. 'I still monitor everything to do with him. I hope one day to be able to ask him if he has any regrets.'

'Well, time's on your side, Hamlet. He's going to be in there for the rest of his life.'

'I sometimes feel as though it's me who got the life sentence. I had to leave my beautiful home and now I've ended up here, very much a prisoner like him. The place is even rigged with cameras like where he is.'

'Yes, but those were put in after what happened to Kieran Croft. They were for your own security. And you wouldn't be without your guard dog,' she said with a grin.

'Oh yes. Lucky will certainly give someone a nasty nip if they come snooping.'

They both let out a laugh.

Hamlet held out a hand. 'Come on, let me top that glass up for you. Then I'll get changed and rustle us up some food. I don't know about you but I'm famished and there's two ten-ounce sirloin steaks back there with our names on them.'

NINE

The next morning Hamlet awoke before 6 a.m., showered and dressed so as not to wake Alix in the spare room. He whispered 'walk' to Lucky, opened the French doors and watched the little dog bolt out onto the veranda and down the steps to the clearing.

He noted a stillness in the woods this morning. The only sound he could hear was birdsong. He loved mornings like this and under normal circumstances would have spent a lazy hour strolling through his kingdom, but today he wasn't blessed with time. He steered Lucky to the old Roman ruins, where he let him ferret around the ancient smallholding, before returning to the cabin, just as Alix was emerging from her bedroom. She was dressed for work, scrunching her damp hair in a towel.

'This is becoming a habit,' she said with a smile.

For a moment he latched on to her warm eyes. They had both been through so much together these past nine months that it had caused a bond between them that only they understood. From once hating her, he had developed a fondness for her that had only grown in strength since she had saved him from the clutches of death. Suddenly conscious he was holding her gaze for too long, he broke eye contact and replied, 'It's a good job I don't have neighbours. They'd be starting a rumour about us.'

She laughed. 'Thank you for last night. I needed that. The steak was lovely and so was the wine. It's so relaxing here.'

'In spite of the things I said last night, feeling sorry for myself, I have to admit it's a bonus living here. I can certainly switch off once I get home.'

'Well, you'll certainly need it now you're a detective. You're going to be dealing with some pretty gruesome things over the next few years, and you'll need a place like this to keep your sanity.'

Hamlet headed into the kitchen where he put down food and water for Lucky, filled the kettle and put bread into the toaster. 'Talking about rumours, I'll let you go off ahead and then set off after so we don't arrive at work at the same time.'

'Good minds think alike. There's nothing worse than a rumour in this job. And, after all, I'm your supervisor. Mentioning no names, but I know one person who'd make a comment about me favouring you.'

'Nate?'

She grinned. 'You've got him worked out already.'

'Not too difficult. I don't think he's impressed with me turning up in the same department as the one that investigated me.'

'He'll get over it. I don't think it's just you. I think there's a bit of jealousy there involving me. It's not the first time I've seen him like this. Nate and I go a long way back. He was on my shift when I first joined. I think he fancied me at the time but I didn't fancy him. And still don't. Also, it hasn't helped that we were partners before I got promoted and we went on the same promotion board for the sergeant post and I got the job, so there's also a bit of bitterness towards me as well.'

'Oh dear.'

'Oh dear exactly. Anyway, that's his problem. Don't let him get to you. I don't.' She finished drying her hair and returned the towel to the bathroom. When she came back Hamlet handed her a mug of coffee and two slices of toast.

Lauren opened morning briefing by telling everyone that they had found footage of Hayley's last known movements, explaining that the clip she was going to show them had been captured by a static camera positioned on the corner of a building opposite the Doctor's Orders pub.

She played it on the large interactive whiteboard, starting at the point where it picked up Hayley on the footpath outside the pub. In the background, standing by the front door of the pub, two men and a woman were huddled together chatting and smoking. The time in the bottom right corner read 23.53.

Hamlet studied the footage. He knew from earlier briefings that he was witnessing Hayley waiting for the taxi she had ordered, and according to the driver designated to pick her up, he had got there at a few minutes after midnight and there had been no sign of her. *This is a key moment in the investigation*, he thought to himself.

At 23.54 the three smokers stubbed out their cigarettes, the woman stole a brief glance at Hayley and then all three trooped back inside the pub, the doors closing behind them. One minute later twin beams of light briefly illuminated Hayley and she shot her gaze in their direction, following the lights as they arced across her body and then vanished in the direction of Northumberland Road.

Unfortunately the camera's angle didn't pick up the car nor was it able to track it's movement. For the next few seconds Hayley stood motionless, though it looked as if she was shouting in the direction the car had travelled. She pulled her phone from her back jeans pocket, checked the screen briefly — Hamlet guessed she was looking at the time — and then set off at a jog away out of shot of camera. The time was 23.55.

Lauren froze the footage and said, 'Was that vehicle a taxi? It's certainly got a reaction from her, and we know it wasn't one from the firm she called because we've been able to track that and we have a statement from the driver who should have picked her up. If it was a black cab it wasn't a Sheffield-based one because we've traced all those and spoken with the drivers. What we do know is that on that road her damaged phone and driving licence were discovered the next morning.' Aiming the remote at the screen she added, 'Find that vehicle and I think we'll have found who took Hayley. Sadly, we have no other CCTV along Northumberland Road that picks up traffic movement. This is our only footage at the moment.'

The clip was played again, Lauren inviting comment, but no one said anything. Hamlet knew it was a lead but not one that could take them any further and the remainder of the session was taken up with information about Hayley's call data.

The techies had discovered that the crank calls to her mobile had started six weeks before she disappeared. Two unregistered numbers had been detected. One of those had made three calls before she blocked it and two had been made from the other before being blocked. Each of these calls had been exactly one week apart, the last one made at 8.20 p.m. on the evening of her disappearance.

'This was just after Hayley had finished her shift at Pink Rhino. Was our guy following her at this stage?' Lauren asked. 'It certainly is a possibility given that three and a half hours later she vanished. I've tasked the CCTV viewers to look more closely at footage we have found of Hayley walking up West Street from Pink Rhino to Bar One where we know she met up with her friends that night.'

Pointing the remote at the interactive screen Lauren closed down the CCTV footage and brought up the photograph of 20-year-old Jessica McKenna. 'We also know from Jessica's phone data that she also received two calls from the same unregistered number as the one that made the first three calls to Hayley. And before that Jessica also received four calls from another unregistered number that has now been deactivated.

'As with Hayley's, each of these calls came exactly one week apart, the last being around the time she caught the tram from Ponds Forge to Centertainment on the evening of her disappearance. And as you also know both Hayley and Jessica each received an identical wedding invitation.

'Not only is that a positive link between both women but we also have a call made to both women's phones from the same unregistered number hours before they went missing. This has to be the same individual involved.

'Hamlet has pointed out that he believes there will have been others before Jessica and Hayley and I'm inclined to believe that so I've tasked him with checking missing persons who fit the profile of Hayley and Jessica. If he comes up with any names, I want those following up with immediate effect. In the meantime, it's imperative we follow up any leads that may point us in the direction of where Hayley and Jessica might be.'

Something was gnawing away at Hamlet. He had worked his way through the dozen files he had gathered of young women in their early twenties who had gone missing in the Sheffield area but not one of the dossiers had triggered anything, and as he closed the last folder it dawned on him why. He had rushed the job. He had been so keen to come up with something for the investigation that he had crammed in the reading of each one without taking stock of their content.

Pushing back his chair he let out an exasperated sigh and then took a deep breath. He had just wasted two hours. As he looked at the casefiles he knew the only way to approach this was in the same methodical way he had studied each of his patients' files before beginning his assessment of them, making salient notes as he went along.

He pushed his laptop and keyboard to the back of his desk, creating as much desk space as he could, and then placed each file next to one another, flipping open their covers.

The first thing he selected from each record was the photograph of the missing woman and he placed this above their file. Then he set about ensuring that each of the file's contents were put in the same order, commencing with the original missing person report and following that with family and friend statements. Happy with that, he returned to looking at the photographs of the missing women and decided to approach the task in hand by first selecting those women who had similarities of likeness to Hayley and Jessica, thereby posing the question, did their abductor have a chosen type?

He also wanted to check whether any of these missing women were students at the university. Casting his eyes along the string of photographs he began his assignment by selecting those with long dark hair, switching their files to the front of the queue. He had seven as a starting point.

It was gone 4 p.m. by the time Hamlet closed the last folder. By then he had absorbed the contents of each file, made half-a-dozen phone calls, and written a pile of notes, only breaking three times; twice to make himself a coffee and once to nip down to the canteen where he had grabbed a ham and cheese sandwich and returned straight to his desk.

As he checked his watch and glanced at the incident board displaying Hayley Stevenson's and Jessica McKenna's timeline, he picked up three of the folders, pushed back his chair and took a look over the desk divide. He saw Alix was hammering away at her keyboard. 'Have you got twenty minutes, Alix?' he asked, slipping around the side of his desk.

She looked up. 'Sure, I'm just putting together our statements for the other night. Have you got something?'

'I think I have. I want to run these past you and get your thoughts,' Hamlet replied, holding up the three folders he'd chosen. He scooted his chair around the side of his desk and laid the files in front of her. He picked up the first folder and flicked back the cover. 'First things first. Looking at our missing women, Hayley and Jessica, there are multiple things each of them have in common.

'They are both in their early twenties. They are slim with long dark hair in a similar style. And they are both students at Sheffield University. They both received anonymous calls from unregistered mobiles, where the male speaker said similar things, according to our witnesses. And we know the same number rang both of them. And finally, they both received anonymous wedding invitations.' Seeing Alix nod, he continued, 'So taking into account each of those parallels, I have picked out these three women from the dozen I got off the missing persons index yesterday. The first is twenty-year-old Molly Fraser. She has been missing the longest.' He pointed at her photograph. 'As you can see, she fits Hayley and Jessica's physical profile and age. And she was also a student at Sheffield Uni at the time of her disappearance.'

Catching Alix's curious look, and smiling to himself because he knew he had her attention, he continued, 'Molly went missing four years ago, in January 2017. She lived with her parents in the village of Ughill, near Bradfield. According to her parents' statement's she'd got her place at uni during the summer of 2016 and had decided to live at home because she had her own car and could drive easily into Sheffield for lectures, do the majority of her work in the library during the day, and then come home late afternoon, unless she was meeting up with friends.

'She occasionally stayed in Sheffield at a friend's flat if they were going out into the city at night but there was nothing regular in those arrangements. She'd had a couple of boyfriends in her mid-teens, but she was not in a relationship at the time of her disappearance.

'On the day she went missing she set off for university shortly after nine. According to her mum's statement she had two lectures that day, the first at 10.30 a.m. and the second at two. She didn't expect her back until around four.

'It had been snowing overnight, but not heavily, and by the time Molly set off several vehicles had cut a path through the narrow roads good enough for travel into the city with careful driving. However, it would appear that two miles outside the village, just before she got to Stacey Bank, she skidded and crashed into the stone walling close to the reservoir. Another car was following and saw the crash.

'The driver was an ambulanceman on his way into work and he stopped to see if she was all right. She told him she was, and he saw that her car had a damaged front wheel and was well and truly stuck, which he pointed it out to her, and she told him she was going to ring her dad and get him to come and help. He checked with her again to see if she was okay, and happy she didn't need medical attention, carried on to his work.

'On the way he decided to give the police a call and inform them about the accident because part of Molly's car was still on the road and he didn't want anyone to crash into it. The police went to have a look, arriving twenty minutes later. They found the car locked up and Molly gone, and assumed she had been picked up by her dad.

'Phone records show that Molly contacted her father at 9.24 and left him a voicemail message because he was in a meeting. At 9.26 she rang her mum and spoke with her. She told her she'd bumped her car but not to panic, she was unhurt, and that she had got a lift in to uni. She said she'd ring her about three p.m. to get a lift back home.

'That was the last time she called. She never turned up at uni. Her tutor received an email via Molly's phone, timed at 10.13, telling him that she would have to miss the lecture because she had crashed her car and couldn't get in. Her phone data shows that it went offline shortly after that email was sent and the phone hasn't been used since.'

Alix lifted her eyes from Molly's photograph. Tight-lipped she said, 'What about the scene of the crash? Any sign of a struggle?'

Hamlet shook his head. 'Not according to the report. Only one set of footprints in the snow around the car, which looked like Molly's. The car was recovered and except for the damage to the front nearside wheel it was clean of any suspicious forensics. A full search of the area was made, including around the reservoir, but no sign was found of her. The last known person to see her was the ambulance driver. He was interviewed, but he didn't recall seeing anyone around when he left her by the side of the road. He clocked on for his ten a.m. shift at the Hallamshire and worked through until six p.m. There is no indication in the report that he is a suspect.'

'What about similarities with Hayley's and Jessica's disappearances? Any mysterious phone calls, complaints of stalking or receiving a wedding invitation?'

'There's nothing in the file to suggest she received a wedding invitation or made a complaint to anyone about stalking, but there is a copy of her phone record in the file, though none of the numbers on there have been highlighted to indicate unusual activity. I have got a name of a detective from the file. She was working at Stocksbridge CID when the missing report was filed but I haven't done anything to contact her at the moment. I was waiting for instructions before doing that.'

'So, the only link with Molly to our two missing women is that she's the same age, same physical characteristics and that she attended Sheffield Uni?'

'For now, yes.'

'Okay, Hamlet, she's a maybe for now then. We'll need to speak with the detective who worked on her case. I'll get the boss to okay us doing some follow-up enquiries.'

Hamlet nodded.

'What about these other two?'

Hamlet turned over the cover of his second file and slid out a photograph of 21-year-old Sophie Booker. Like Hayley, Jessica and Molly, Sophie was pretty, had long dark hark and was slim. Her photo showed her looking relaxed and smiling, and the background suggested it had been taken at some kind of function.

Sophie had disappeared in June 2018. She hailed from the Broom Valley area of Rotherham, lived with her parents and younger brother and was about to take her summer break after completing her first year at Sheffield University studying digital media.

On the evening of the 16th, a Saturday, Sophie had arranged to meet up with a group of friends at a pub on the outskirts of Rotherham, where they were going to spend a few hours drinking and then catch a taxi into Rotherham where they would tour the late-night bars before sharing a taxi back to their respective homes.

Sophie was dropped off at the pub by her dad just after seven and for the next three hours the group of four drank a variety of drinks including shots, booking a taxi for 10.30 p.m. to take them into Rotherham to visit more bars.

Each of Sophie's friends said in their statements that they had all had a fair bit to drink, but that they were just merry by the time their taxi was due. The taxi had been ordered on Sophie's phone and they all said that she received a text five minutes before the time she'd booked it informing her it was on its way.

Sophie had almost finished her drink while the others still had some way to go, so she drank up and said she'd go out to the car park and wait for it and then call them so that it wouldn't drive off.

At 10.27 one of the women received a call from Sophie's mobile. She answered, telling Sophie 'They were all coming' and ended the call without waiting for her to respond. When they went out to the car park there was no sign of Sophie and no sign of the taxi.

As they were about to call the taxi firm to see why the taxi had only taken Sophie, a taxi turned up for them and when they quizzed the driver about their pick-up, he said that he was the one who had been given the job, and that their company did not send texts to notify customers prior to being picked up.

The women tried ringing Sophie's phone but each time it diverted to voicemail. After ten minutes of making frantic phone calls to her, they called the police. A later check of Sophie's phone record showed that the text message supposedly from the taxi company came from an unregistered mobile and Sophie's phone went offline immediately after her call to her friend at 10.27.

'And I guess we never found out the owner of the unregistered mobile?' said Alix as Hamlet closed Sophie Booker's folder.

Hamlet shook his head.

'Is it among any of the unregistered numbers received by Hayley or Jessica?'

'Nope.'

'Is it listed more than once on Molly Fraser's phone log?'

'She has a long list. I've run through it once and not noticed the number, but I confess I haven't done a thorough line-by-line check of her phone data.'

'Okay, that's something we can do. Did Sophie mention to her friends or anyone else about receiving any unwanted calls or complain about being stalked?'

'If she did, it's not in the file. And there's no mention of a wedding invitation. I've made a note of the officers involved and there's a phone number for Sophie's parents, but I've held off contacting anyone at this stage.'

'So, in Sophie's case, we again have only two similar factors. The same physical characteristics and that she went to Sheffield Uni.'

'Like I say, I haven't spoken with any of the case officers yet, or the parents or witnesses and asked them those relevant questions.'

'Well, these two are worth making those checks. For now, they're both a maybe. Now run the last one past me.'

Hamlet turned over the cover of the third folder. 'Twenty-year-old Madison Yates from Sheffield. And also at Sheffield Uni,' he began, picking up her photo and handing it to Alix. 'As you can see, she had the same physical appearance as the others. If the same person abducted these women, it's not difficult to see he has a type.'

The photograph of Madison showed her sitting in a hammock chair wearing what looked like pyjamas. She had a laptop resting on one thigh and was laughing at the camera, her dark brown hair cascading around her face.

'Madison disappeared two and a bit years ago, nine months before Jessica McKenna, but there's an anomaly in her disappearance.'

'Anomaly?' Alix interjected, lifting her gaze.

'According to this record, a former boyfriend went to jail for two years for assaulting her and a friend of hers. That assault happened a few weeks before she disappeared, and I'll get on to that, but first I'll tell you about the circumstances of her disappearance.

'Two and a half years ago she was at a house party with friends, when her boyfriend, a guy called Jack Bennett, turned up, begging her to withdraw the statement she'd made about him assaulting her several weeks prior. There was a heated argument between them, during which other members of the party got involved, and there was a bit of a tussle and the police were called.

'Jack left before they arrived, making threats to Madison, but she wouldn't complain to the police when they attended, and so they left and it was written off as a disturbance.

'Shortly after one a.m. she and a friend left and set off walking home. Their walk wasn't a long one, less than a mile. Madison and her friend lived four streets away from one another, the friend's house being the closest. Her friend said that Madison was a little bit drunk and upset by what had happened with Jack and they chatted about it on the way home and outside her gate for a few minutes. Then they said goodnight to one another and her friend watched her walk away to the corner of the street.

That was the last time she was seen. She was reported missing in the early hours by her parents. Jack, the ex-boyfriend, was spoken to the next morning, where he admitted arguing and threatening Madison at the party, but said that as soon as he heard the police had been called, he high-tailed it away with a mate, who dropped him off at the flat where he was staying, where he ended up smoking cannabis with the flatmate until he crashed out about three a.m.

'Jack was interviewed three times and gave the same story every time. He was kept in custody for forty-eight hours during which they spoke to his flatmate, who confirmed everything Jack said. This report states that there wasn't enough evidence to charge and so he was released; however, Jack remains the main suspect in Madison's abduction.'

'So why have you included her?'

'There are several things that don't add up. True, Jack Bennett did beat Madison Yates up after she dumped him, which was witnessed by a friend who he also assaulted, but with regards her abduction, all police have is circumstantial evidence. And there are statements in this file that challenge that he was the only suspect in her abduction. For instance, a couple of her friends said that several weeks before Madison was assaulted by Jack, she told them someone was repeatedly phoning her, telling her that he loved her and wanted her, and she'd blocked the calls. And she also told them this person was sending her stuff, but it hasn't been elaborated in their statements what that "stuff" was. And there's also this I've found on the internet.'

From the back of the file, Hamlet pulled out two sheets of paper. They were print-outs of the front and inside pages of *The Retford Record* newspaper bearing the headline **INNOCENT.** Beside the headline was a picture of a blonde-haired woman in her late forties holding up a framed photograph of a brown-haired boy in his late teens, wearing a T-shirt. His well-toned arms were heavily sleeved with tattoos. The caption beneath it stated, *Debra Bennett says her son Jack, 22, is innocent over the disappearance of 20-year-old Madison Yates from Sheffield.*

'In a nutshell, Jack Bennett's mum alleges that detectives tried to frame her son for Madison's disappearance because he'd been in trouble with the police and suffers from ADHD. It basically gives a bit of background about Jack who lives with his mum in Retford following his release from prison, saying he was expelled from school and got into trouble over smoking cannabis at fifteen but turned his life around when he got a job as a mechanic at a local garage.

'Two years previously, he transferred to a bigger branch in Sheffield, where he met Madison who worked there as a part-time receptionist and they started going out together. His mother states that the reason Madison split with her son was because her parents thought she was too good for him and that caused several rows between them which brought about the break-up. She also states that they falsely complained to the police about him harassing her, and that her friends exaggerated the assault that got him jailed. The article says that Madison's parents have refused to comment, as do the police.'

'Do you know, Hamlet, I remember this case now. It was on the telly and in the local paper. It was dealt with by Ecclesfield CID where she lived. I remember that the team who worked on it were convinced that Jack was responsible for her disappearance and I'm guessing that's the reason why they haven't responded to the article. It's probably still an open case and it could prejudice things. And we always ask the complainant, in this case Madison's parents, not to comment.'

Hamlet returned an understanding nod. 'There's a few paragraphs in the missing report about how Madison and Jack first got together but within three months she was tiring of him because he was becoming too possessive and she didn't like his use of cannabis. And in Madison's parents' statements there's reference to a number of arguments they witnessed when he came to the house after she had broken off their relationship, and also some phone calls he made threatening her.

'The assault on Madison happened in a bar on West Street. Jack turned up on a Friday night two weeks before she disappeared in a drunken state and mouthing off. She shoved him away and he thumped her in the face, breaking her cheekbone, busting her nose and mouth. Her friends intervened and he assaulted one of them, and then door staff restrained him until the police arrived.

'It was all captured on CCTV. He was charged with the assault on Madison and her friend, and then bailed and released. According to her parents, after he was released, he made a series of phone calls to Madison, initially apologising for his behaviour and trying to persuade her to withdraw her complaint, but when she wouldn't, he threatened her. Her parents tried persuading her to make a complaint about the threatening calls but she wouldn't.

'Then, as I've already explained, we have the party where Jack again tried to get her to drop the assault, and a few hours later she disappeared. Jack had made two phone calls to Madison's mobile that night before he turned up at the party, and he was locked up for forty-eight hours before being released without charge after continuing to deny being involved in her disappearance. Hence the newspaper article.' Hamlet tapped the print-outs of the *Retford Record* as he finished. 'I think the mysterious phone calls and the stuff she was sent should have been followed up. To me it looks like that the officer who dealt with this had made up their mind that Jack Bennett was responsible for Madison Yates' disappearance and run with it. I think we need to get to the bottom of the phone calls and find out exactly what was the stuff she was sent before we discount her from the list.'

TEN

Hamlet slammed down the desk phone handset.

Alix rose and peered over the divider. 'Someone annoying you, Hamlet?' she asked, a smirk dancing across her face.

'I've just had a DS at Ecclesfield give me a right earbashing over Jack Bennett. Asked me what experience I'd got, and then telling me when I'd got in as much time as he had then I could start criticising. I wouldn't mind but I only asked if they were absolutely confident it was Jack who'd abducted Madison, or if they had someone else it could possibly be. He asked me whose side I was on and that I sounded just like CPS, who'd refused to charge him.'

Alix let out a laugh. 'What did the boss tell you about sceptics and cynics? Look at it from his point of view. You're a trainee detective, two minutes in the job and you're questioning how he's worked for the past ten or twenty years. He's probably one of those that was around when they could bend the rules to suit.'

'If I hadn't been told I had to respect the rank I'd have given him both barrels talking to me like that. There isn't a shred of solid evidence that Jack abducted Madison. It's all circumstantial.'

'I'm on your side, Hamlet, but we don't always get the solid evidence we want. Sometimes all we have is circumstantial. And you have to agree there's plenty of that with Jack. Like you say, he threatened Madison when they split up, then he follows her to a pub where he assaults her. He threatens her again when she won't drop her complaint, and on the day she disappeared, he admits going to a party where he knows she is and threatening her again, and hours later she disappears.

'His only alibi is that a mate drove him back to the flat he was sharing, and he won't tell detectives who that person is. Sure enough, his flatmate confirms Jack was there until at least three a.m. when he crashed out after smoking cannabis, but it's only his word. There are no independent witnesses that can corroborate his movements.

'There was no forensic evidence linking him to Madison on the clothing he was wearing, and he didn't have a vehicle or access to any vehicle to take her away. Did you manage to ask the DS what they took as evidence?'

'Yes. They took her laptop and mobile. I asked him if there were any calls to her mobile from an unregistered mobile and he confirmed there were five to her. They never traced the number. They searched Jack's mate's flat, his workplace, and his mother's house in Retford but all they recovered was Jack's phone that was registered to him on a contract.'

'Did the DS say if Madison's case was still open?'

'He said it was. Of sorts. He says they've exhausted all their enquiries. Oh, and he told me Jack went back to live with his mum at Retford after he got out of prison.'

'Well, I'll tell you what we'll do then. You make the call to Doncaster Prison and check if Jack was definitely inside when Jessica McKenna disappeared, and I'll clear it with the gaffer to go and pay him a visit at Retford. Let's see what impression we have of him after a little chat.'

Jack Bennett and his mum, Debra, lived in the Westfield area of Retford, close to the wharf. The terrace row of houses were Victorian, the brickwork grimy from past years of smoke-filled streets and that morning they looked even more dour in the rain-filled mist. Alix rapped on the uPVC door.

It took a second knock before a woman opened the door a fraction and poked her head through the gap. Alix instantly recognised her from the newspaper piece. As the door opened a little further, she caught a whiff of cannabis. She guessed from what they knew about Jack that he was probably having a spliff and had quickly ditched it.

'Oh, it's you lot. At least you haven't kicked the bloody door down this time,' Debra said gruffly, opening the door further. She stuck her head out into the street and gazed up and down. When she saw that Alix and Hamlet were the only people about, she said, 'Just seeing if there were any nosy bleeders about. It's probably one of these grassing fuckers that have got our Jack put inside again.'

'Your Jack's locked up?' Alix asked.

'Yeah.' She let the word out slowly as if they were stupid. 'Two days ago. As if you didn't know.'

'I didn't. We're not local. We're from South Yorks. We came here for a chat with Jack.'

'And you lot are just as bad as well. It was you that locked him up the last time. And you've been harassing him ever since he got out. Well, you're too late. He's gone back in for breaking his licence. They said they'll be charging him with supplying. It's only a bit of cannabis for fuck's sake.'

Alix bit her tongue because she needed to talk to Debra about Jack. She also guessed, from what his mother had just gesticulated, that the damage to her door was from a recent drugs raid. His mother was most probably smoking some of his stash the police hadn't found. Or her own.

'What do you want this time?' Then, as if reading Alix's mind, 'There're no more drugs here. You got them all when you busted Jack.'

Alix put her foot against the front door, more a statement that she wanted to talk inside than prevent Debra from closing it in their faces. 'Now I know that's strictly not true because I could smell cannabis the moment you opened the door, but I can assure you, Debra, we are not here to discuss your smoking habits, all we want is to ask you a few questions about Jack and his relationship with Madison Yates.'

'This is what I'm talking about. Harassing him again,' she huffed. 'Our Jack's already done time because of her and her snobby parents. He had nothing to do with her going missing. How many times do you need telling? If you ask me you need to speak to her parents. They're the ones who are possessive.'

'Look, Mrs Bennett, we're not the detectives who were involved when your Jack assaulted Madison. We're from a team who're taking a fresh look at Madison's disappearance. We might be actually doing him, and you, a favour by asking you these questions. What you say we talk inside?'

'You're not here to harass us?'

Alix shook her head. 'Just a chat, that's all.'

'Okay, but if there's any funny business, you two can make one. I've already been to the papers about you accusing my Jack about Madison going missing when he's nowt to do with it.'

'No funny business at all, Mrs Bennett,' Alix replied, and Debra opened the door to allow them in.

The room was dim, the lack of daylight because the curtains were half closed, though Alix couldn't help but think that the dimness hid the dirty state it was in. Most of the room was taken up with a chunky green leather three-piece suite, the hide stained and one side panel of the sofa ripped with stuffing poking through. The only other items of furniture were a 50-inch flat screen TV and a glass-top coffee table in the middle of the room, it's surface ring-marked with tea or coffee stains. It had an empty pizza box on it with an overflowing ashtray. Some of the tab-ends were the remains of spliffs. Debra wasn't even trying to conceal her drug use. Alix couldn't help but think of her son Jack, sat in his prison cell, probably looking at another couple of years inside, and told herself that he never really had a chance in life with a mother like this.

Debra dropped into a chair, the cushion sinking beneath her weight. 'Park your arses then and ask your questions.'

Alix took one look at the state of the sofa and said, 'It's okay, Debra. To be honest we're up to our necks in it. We're also dealing with two other missing women in Sheffield. You might have heard about them and seen it on the telly. We're here because Madison's disappearance might be connected to them and that's why we want this chat. Just to clear up a few things about Jack.'

Debra suddenly pushed herself forward. 'Just a minute. Are you trying to fit-up our Jack for some more women going missing?'

Alix shook her head. 'No, Mrs Bennett, I'm not saying that. The reason we're here is to try and clear up once and for all what Jack was doing on the day Madison disappeared.'

'He told those detectives who questioned him.'

'I don't think he told them everything. He turned up at a party Madison was attending just hours before she disappeared, threatening her. He told detectives that a mate drove him back to the flat where he was staying, but he wouldn't tell them who that mate was. We only have his word for what happened around the time Madison disappeared. We can't account for two and a half hours between him leaving the party after threatening Madison and him crashing out at the flat he was sharing with his mate.' Alix paused and watched her for a reaction, but Debra remained poker-face. She continued, 'Now I know he was asked this when he was questioned, and I'm guessing they also asked you, did he have a car, or access to one, when he was going out with Madison?'

She got a reaction then.

Debra dropped her gaze, but it was for only a split second. Eyeing Alix, she replied, 'You're asking me that because you know he was working at the garage when he was going with her, aren't you? Well, I can tell you, he didn't drive any of the cars from there. Not one. He liked that job. I know he could drive, but he hasn't passed his test, which he told his boss, so they would only let him work on them.' In that moment her face took on a worried look.

Hamlet spotted it and jumped in with, 'Is there something worrying you, Debra? Do you mind if I call you Debra? Do you know something about your son that's troubling you?'

She answered softly, 'Look, I'm worried about our Jack. He could have put a stop to this, but he's scared. Our Jack can prove he had nothing to do with Madison going missing.'

'How can he do that? In what way, Debra?' Hamlet pressed.

'If he told you, it would mean he has to grass some people up and he's worried about being accused of being a snitch. He could also get them jailed.'

Alix took back the conversation, 'Look, Mrs Bennett, we can't give up on this until we are happy that Jack wasn't involved in Madison's disappearance. If it means someone getting into trouble to stop Jack being accused, then surely he should think of himself. And if you know he's innocent, like you say he is, then surely you should think about saying something in his place. It's the best way of helping Jack. And it could help us find out what happened to Madison. I know you're not fond of her or her parents, but if she was your daughter what would you want?'

Debra's eyes darted from Alix to Hamlet and back. After a period of silence she said, 'Look, this hasn't come from me. Okay?'

'If it can help your Jack, it's worth telling us.'

'That night after he argued with Madison, he left the party and went straight round to his dealer's place to buy some skunk. That's what he and his flatmate got stoned on. He bought twenty pound's worth from him.'

'And where does his dealer live?' asked Alix.

'I don't know an address or his name. I've only got a phone number for him.'

'Detectives took Jack's phone. There wasn't any activity on it between him leaving Madison's and getting back to his mate's flat.'

'That's because he switched it off and used a mate's phone. Look, that night, Jack had fixed up to pick up his gear and also get some for someone his mate knew. It was this other friend that drove him, first to the party and then to the dealer's place where he scored and then they went back to Jack's mate's flat for a smoke. The other friend left before the police turned up asking about Madison going missing and Jack decided to keep him out of it. This friend is from a decent family, our Jack says, and has never been in any trouble. He didn't want to dob him in, and he's too scared to tell you lot anything about his dealer.'

'So, there are two other people who would be able to vouch for Jack's movements after he left the party Madison had attended?' Alix asked.

Debra nodded, shuffling uncomfortably. 'This hasn't come from me, okay?'

Hamlet placed the receiver back on his desk phone and peered over the divider to Alix. 'Well, that's Jack Bennett cleared of Madison Yates' disappearance,' he announced, grabbing her attention.

'Alibied?' she asked, looking up from her computer.

'Cast iron, you could say, unless his mates are involved as well. As Jack's mum said, the friend has never been in trouble before. His name's Ryan Mellor. He's twenty-four and works for the same garage as Jack did. He's in the finance section. I've just got off the phone to him. He was extremely nervous and more than helpful in coming forward with his story. He's crapping himself that his boss or parents might find out about the cannabis. He swears he isn't a regular user and told me it was Jack who got him into it after sharing a spliff with him one night when they went into town.

'As you can imagine, threatened with that, it wasn't hard to get him to talk. He told me that on the night Jack went to the party to try and persuade Madison to withdraw her complaint, Jack phoned him and asked for a lift to the party and in return he'd give him a bag of skunk. Ryan knew Jack had split up with Madison, and about him assaulting her, and he told me that Jack was bricking it because his solicitor had told him that the likelihood was that he would get a custodial sentence, so he wanted to try and get her to drop the charge.

'Ryan confirms he drove Jack to the party at Ecclesfield and waited for him in the car while he went to speak with her. He said Madison kept him standing on the doorstep and he saw the pair getting into a heated argument and then everything kicked off with Jack and a couple of the lads from the party, and that Jack came back fuming, telling him the cops had been called and they needed to get out of there.

'Ryan didn't need any persuading and told me he thought he was driving Jack straight back to his mate's flat but then Jack told him that he needed to get stoned and to drive him to his dealer's place. Ryan told me he was extremely nervous because it wasn't his scene at all but he drove him to Parkhill flats where the dealer lived, waited for him while he bought twenty-quid's worth of cannabis, and then drove him back to Jack's other mate's flat, where they all smoked a spliff. He left the flat around one-thirty in the morning alone and drove straight home. He says both Jack and his mate were well on their way to being stoned when he left.'

'It looks as though Jack is clear after all. And it looks like Madison is one to add to our missing list, smarty-pants.'

Hamlet gave a triumphant grin. 'I think it does. And on that front, I've done a few quick enquiries of Madison's phone log with regards unregistered calls, and she received six calls from two unknown numbers which were no longer than thirty seconds, but shortly after midnight on the night she disappeared she received a phone call from a third unknown number, and she was on the phone for almost two minutes.'

'That's about an hour before she left the party. And she's on the phone for two minutes? That's a long time speaking with someone on an unregistered number. Does that mean she knew who she was talking to?'

'Well, she certainly didn't end the call as quickly as the others. Someone managed to keep the call going.'

'And you've traced the number?'

Hamlet nodded. 'It's disconnected.'

Alix shook her head slowly, a disconsolate look on her face. 'Whoever's taking these women, Hamlet, is certainly not leaving any trace of themselves.'

'He will have left a trace. We just haven't found it yet. I think we're only just at the tip of the iceberg with these latest three women. The oldest went missing almost four years ago. I think we need to either look for others, maybe not in this area, and even go back a lot further in time. Whoever's involved seems to have developed a well-practised procedure with these disappearances, so he must have done a rehearsal and made a mistake. That's how we catch him.'

ELEVEN

It was early when Alix rang Hamlet. He was still in the woods on his morning walk with Lucky when she phoned.

'Get your running shoes on, Hamlet, Hayley's been found. The boss has just rung me. They found her a couple of hours ago in an old MOD bunker at Low Bradfield. She was unconscious and in a bad way but she's alive. She's been rushed to the Hallamshire and uniform are babysitting her. As soon as I hang up I'm going to contact Katie and Nick and get them to go straight there to see how she is and see if they can get anything from her. I'm just on my way to join Lauren and Nate at the scene and I want you to join us. You need to see how we work a crime scene. How long will you be?'

Alix had machine-gunned the information, not giving Hamlet any time to respond. As she finished, he replied, 'Probably three-quarters of an hour. I'm with Lucky in the woods. I'm on my way back to the cabin and I need to get changed but I'll get there as fast as I can. Can you send me the coordinates? I know Low Bradfield is mainly made up of farms but it's so spread out I might have difficulty finding you.'

'Nate tells me it's like Fred Karno's circus. He and the boss are getting things organised. I'll text you the location and see you there.'

Hamlet nipped in with, 'Do you think sending Nick to the hospital is a good idea, Alix? Considering it's more than likely that a man abducted her? You said she's in a bad way. She could well be mentally traumatised as well, and having a man there questioning her could damage her further. I don't want to tell you how to do your job, Alix, but I'd just have Katie there for now. Until Hayley has been properly examined and the doctor tells you what her mental state is like.'

There was a pause down the line and then Alix responded, 'Good point, Hamlet. Thank you. Okay, I'll see you shortly. Oh, and by the way, Nate tells me they've found bodies there as well. He didn't go into detail because he sounded up to his neck. Could be our other missing women. I'll not know until I get there. Hope you're up to this. I don't want you going all squeamish on me.'

He was about to say he'd seen enough dead people as a doctor but Alix had already hung up. Pocketing his phone, Hamlet and Lucky set off at a trot back to the cabin, his thoughts already focussing on what he'd learned at training school about crime scene preservation and the collection of evidence. Just over a week ago he'd been having second thoughts about taking on the role of a detective, but now, as he raced back to get changed, he could see why Alix spoke so fondly about her job — the adrenalin was already beginning to surge.

Hamlet's journey to Low Bradfield took him longer than he anticipated. The most direct route took him through a series of small towns along single-lane roads where traffic was heavy with commuters, so by the time he reached the Bradfield turn-off frustration was eating away at him. However, as he passed the old coaching pub, The Strines Inn, the road opened up, offering stunning views across the Derwent Valley, the huge sky full of scudding white summer clouds, that instantly lifting his mood. He and Helen had frequently visited Bradfield for summer walks around the spectacular reservoirs finishing the day at The Old Horns Inn at High Bradfield, where they took in the beautiful views across the valley with a drink or two before returning home. The pleasant memories were bittersweet, knowing he would never experience them again.

Through High Bradfield the roads were narrow and tight in places but there was no congestion and he cleared the rural hamlet easily. His Sat Nav prompted him that his destination was only a mile away and he put his foot down again. A quarter of a mile along the road he spotted a signpost for Ughill which immediately triggered a memory from his recent enquiries. Molly Fraser had lived there. That was too much of a coincidence. *Was one of the bodies hers?*

His next landmark was a farm to his right, and as he crested the rise he saw his destination ahead, the route lined by at least a dozen vehicles, some police and some civilian, and he started to slow. A man was climbing out of one of the civilian cars and Hamlet recognised the *Sheffield Telegraph* reporter who'd caused furore at the press conference. Driving on, he came to the marked police vehicles where he pulled in front of a large forensics van and stopped.

Thankfully he had brought along his waterproof jacket and although the mild weather didn't warrant it he put it on, pulling up the hood before climbing out of his car. The last thing he wanted right now was the press spotting him. He hadn't yet decided how he was going to handle that one, even though he knew it was going to happen eventually.

Twenty yards away he saw a constable wearing a high-vis jacket standing guard at a gate, a ribbon of blue and white tape fastened across the entrance, and he hurried towards him over the uneven grass verge. As he neared and looked over the stone wall into the field, he caught his first sight of an active crime scene; a line of half-a-dozen officers dressed in dark blue and wearing baseball caps were steadily walking among the crops.

Beyond them he spotted five people garbed in white forensic suits in a scrum before a large grass mound and he knew he had found the bunker and Alix, Nate, Lauren and two others. He showed his ID to the officer by the gate who pointed out a path to take and he followed it, doing his best not to trample down any more of the leafed crops that had already been flattened by footfall.

As he approached, Alix, Nate and Lauren turned towards him.

'Your timing is perfect, Hamlet,' Lauren said. 'We're just about to go in and see what we've got. Slip your coat off and grab a suit. I hope you haven't had breakfast because I'm told it's not a pretty sight.'

Hamlet needed help getting into his forensic suit, requiring Alix's shoulder to lean on while he put on the overshoes. Once on, not only did he feel constrained but also uncomfortable moving around in his crinkly cocoon as he followed the others into the bunker. Two CSI's — a portly middle-aged man with glasses, and a slim, much younger woman — led the way, lugging their shiny aluminium equipment cases. They entered a long corridor that was surprisingly draughty given its solid concrete construction. The only light came from an arc lamp set on a tripod halfway along the lengthy corridor and eerie shadows played all around as they made their way further into the bowels of the World War Two building.

'We've only got half a dozen lamps for now, Ma'am,' the male CSI officer called back to Lauren. 'So we've had to space them out as best we can. I've asked for some more to be delivered but it'll be a couple of hours at least. The main fuse has been removed from the electrics and the generator is so old we couldn't get it started.'

'I'll get on to the MOD and see if we can get someone here pronto to power up the lighting. We're going to need it,' Lauren replied.

The door at the end of the lengthy corridor took them into a large room where the electrics and generator were and this was also lit by an arc lamp.

'This place is spooky enough with these lamps,' Alix commented. 'Can you image what it must have been like with just headlamps and torches? The guys who found this place must have crapped themselves when they found Hayley and the bodies.'

'They shouldn't have been here in the first place,' said Lauren, 'but we wouldn't have found Hayley if it hadn't been for them breaking into this former military establishment. By the way who's interviewing them?'

'No one yet. I'm going to set Nick on that,' Alix answered. 'We've seized their vehicle and all their gear for examination, just in case they're involved, but the sergeant who was first here is more than happy with their story. And we've got Hayley to speak to.'

'What's happening with her?'

'I've got Katie to check on her status. She's just messaged me. She's not long arrived at the hospital and just liaised with uniform. The doctors are still assessing Hayley. The latest update is that she's malnourished and severely dehydrated so they've put her on a drip. Katie will message me with a further update once she speaks with the consultant.'

'Good. Have we taken Hayley's clothing for forensics?'

'Yes. Uniform have bagged it. But it's not what she was wearing when she disappeared. She was dressed in a jogging top and bottoms when she was found. Even her underwear has gone.'

'Hopefully, we'll find it in here, once we start the search.' Lauren ended the conversation as they came to the end of a second corridor where steps led down to a pair of metal doors that signalled the entrance to the War Room where Hayley had been found.

As the forensic officer pulled the doors open bright light cascaded through the gap. 'We put the majority of the lights in here. This is where they found Hayley and the bodies,' he said as he stepped inside.

Hamlet was the last one in, joining his colleagues who had come to an abrupt halt in a line several feet inside the room. Four powerful arc lamps on tripods lit up the entire room, and as Hamlet formed up beside the team, he tried to make sense of the tableau illuminated before them.

The scene instantly reminded him of the inside of a small chapel. Two dozen chairs had been placed in three rows, four chairs to each row, evenly separated either side of an aisle. On the front row were seated four female figures in two pairs either side of the aisle, their backs to him, each one dressed in a white long dress. The heads of the women were all looking forward, their faces turned in the direction of another female figure dressed in a white flowing dress who was sculptured kneeling before a makeshift altar, a wooden cross its centrepiece.

'Unbelievable, isn't it?' Lauren exclaimed. 'It's like something out of Madame Tussauds,' she added, stepping off down the aisle.

Everyone followed. As they came level with the kneeling figure, they came to a stop again and began casting their eyes upon the five figures.

Hamlet instantly recognised the kneeling woman from her photograph on her missing file, even though her eyes were closed. Her head had been set so it was facing the cross on the makeshift altar, her arms pressed close to her chest, hands clutching a posy of white flowers. She was perfectly rigid. 'It's Jessica McKenna,' he blurted, stunned by what he saw.

'Jessica!' Alix gasped. 'From Wybourn?'

'I recognise her from her photo.' Though heavily made-up and paler, she looked no different from the photograph on her file and yet she had last been seen eighteen months ago. Had she only recently been killed? His thoughts went into overdrive, searching the part of his brain that stored his medical know-how, casting his thoughts back to corpses he'd seen as a young doctor. He'd watched post-mortems during his training and the bodies had been in a state of rigor mortis then, but he was sure they couldn't be posed like this without falling over.

He swung his gaze to the other four figures seated on the front row, his eyes dancing rapidly from one to another. These were rigid too, their eyes shut, and like Jessica their faces were caked heavily in make-up giving them an almost mannequin-like appearance. He lingered his gaze over the face of the two to his left. He was certain one of them was Madison Yates. Her photograph and image were still at the forefront of his mind because of their recent enquiries. He turned to Alix, pointed her out and softly said her name.

Alix followed Hamlet's finger, casting her eyes upon the doll-like face. After a few seconds, she said, 'I think you're right. Do you recognise who's next to her?'

His eyes fastened upon the frozen face of the woman next to Madison. 'I'm not sure but I think it could be Sophie Booker.'

'And what about that?' Lauren asked, pointing at the wall behind the makeshift altar.

Hamlet had been aware of the writing halfway up the wall behind the altar when he had first entered the room but his attention had been on the bodies. Now he dragged his attention back to it.

TILL DEATH DO US PART had been painted in large black letters and looked to have been done hastily. Some of the letters had run. As he read the words from the traditional wedding vows a shiver ran down Hamlet's back.

Lauren said, 'What kind of person are we dealing with here?'

Turning sharply, Hamlet replied, 'There is no doubt we are looking for a very disturbed individual, boss.' His thoughts spiralled away to James Harry Benson. His killing spree had been driven by revenge, but the person who had done this was not of the same mind as Benson. This was someone who had the ability to be far more controlled, disciplined. And yet he was just as dangerous. Looking at the grim tableau, he added, 'I have no doubt from what we see here that we are looking for someone who is deranged, yet able to present themself as a very affable person.'

'Explain, Hamlet,' said Lauren.

'They are able to plan and think logically. What you see before you is the culmination of all their planning. I have no doubt now that we are looking for someone who has a delusional state of mind. They firmly believe that their victims have feelings for them, and they reciprocate that by bombarding them with messages of love. Abducting them is the culmination of the belief the women want to be with them. Obviously the victims — terrified and desperate — have not returned his affection and so he's killed them. But even then he can't let them go, hence what you see here.'

'The worst thing is, it looks as if we were just a few days too late to save them,' Lauren said quietly.

'I don't think so,' said the female CSI. 'A couple of these women have been dead for some time.'

'What do you mean?' Lauren asked. 'They're heavily made-up, granted, but they look to me as if they've only just been killed.'

'I've taken a closer look,' said the CSI. She was just taking her camera out of her case. 'I might be wrong but I think they've all been embalmed.'

Hamlet recalled the past Popes who had been embalmed after death at the Vatican, and of the visitors who still flocked to see Lenin's preserved body in Moscow's Red Square. Whilst on holiday with Helen in Mexico, the year before they got married, they had gone to see La Pascualita in a wedding store window, rumoured to be the preserved corpse of the former shop owner's daughter who died tragically on her wedding day. As he again ran his eyes over the five corpses, he saw that each one looked to be in the same preserved state as La Pascualita.

'Embalmed! Jesus,' Lauren responded, shaking her head incredulously. Then, 'If three of these women are Jessica McKenna, Madison Yates and Sophie Booker, then who are these other two? Is one of them Molly Fraser?'

Hamlet shook is head. 'I'm not sure at all.'

For a moment they all stared at the seated cadavers, the only sound in the room coming from the click of the digital camera as the CSI officer took photographs.

Suddenly Alix slapped a hand over her mouth, a look of shock on her face, 'No! It can't be!'

TWELVE

Outside Lauren and Hamlet gathered around a hunched-over Alix, who was sucking in deep breaths.

'Do you recognise one of the women?' Lauren asked, gently rubbing the middle of Alix's back.

'I wasn't sure at first because of all the heavy make-up but now I'm certain. I think she's my friend from uni, Elise,' Alix replied, tugging down her facemask and sucking in another deep breath. She held it for a few seconds before letting it out slowly. 'We were in halls together. She had the room next to mine.' She took another deep breath. 'She went missing five years ago. Her parents rang me after she'd disappeared to see if she'd contacted me.' She clapped a hand over her mouth. 'Oh my God. Not Elise.'

'It might not be her, Alix. They're all heavily made-up, as you saw. You could be mistaken,' said Hamlet.

Alix lifted her head and locked eyes with him. 'I know you're only trying to soften the blow, but I'm positive that's Elise. Same build and hair colour, and tied back exactly how she used to wear it. Even with all that make-up I can still make out her face.'

'You say she went missing five years ago?' Lauren asked.

'Yeah.'

'What's her name? Elise what?' Hamlet interjected.

'Elise Farmer now, but it was Elise Lewis when we were at uni. She married a professional photographer seven years ago. I was a bridesmaid at their wedding.'

'How come I didn't see her name among the missing persons?' Hamlet said.

'Because she didn't go missing round here. She was living in North Yorkshire when she disappeared. Her husband, Daniel, is from there and they bought a house out near Grassington. That's where she went missing from. It was her mum who told me she'd gone missing. I was still in uniform back then. She rang me one Saturday and told me Elise had gone missing while out walking. She said she'd gone out with the dog along the river and that some walkers had come across the dog but no sign of her.

'I took the following day off and went up there to see her mum and dad and give them some support. It was awful seeing them like that.' She steadied her breathing before continuing. 'I managed to speak with the inspector in charge and she confessed it was a complete mystery as to what had happened. Elise vanished, just like that. There one minute, gone the next.

'Apparently, she disappeared along a popular walking route, not far from the Tourist Information Centre. They searched for miles nearby, including the river, and it was all over the news. I remember a few people came forward who'd seen her shortly after she'd set off on her walk, but the last sighting of her was about a mile along the trail. Her dog was found fastened to a tree not far from where she'd last been seen.'

'And no suspects?' Lauren asked.

'None as far as I'm aware. They quizzed Daniel a few times but he was photographing a wedding in Skipton the day she disappeared. Lots of people saw him there.' Alix straightened up. The colour had returned to her face. 'Gosh! This is awful. Poor Elise. I always wondered what happened to her, and I have to confess the more time passed the more I suspected she was dead. But how did she get down here? Has she been here all this time?'

'If she has, that could make her our killer's first victim,' Hamlet said.

Lauren and Alix nodded in agreement.

Alix said, 'Five years. We've had a killer operating under our noses all that time and no idea. And my friend Elise was the first. Good God!'

'I know this has come as an almighty shock for you, Alix,' Hamlet said, 'but do you know of anything unusual happening in Elise's life at the time of her disappearance? Any mysterious phone calls or being followed, that type of thing, like with our other victims?'

Alix shook her head. 'We kept in touch for a while after uni, and I knew about her new job, and when she met Daniel. And of course leading up to the wedding, I'd drive up there and stay with her, but then the job got in the way. I went into CID and our calls became less and less frequent, especially the year leading up to her going missing.

'I feel awful now. At uni, we were in rooms next to one another and went everywhere together. Elise was studying journalism and once she graduated she got a job as a junior reporter with the *Sheffield Telegraph* and, because I worked in Sheffield, we were able to keep in touch easily. Weekends out, that kind of thing. Even when she got the post as a reporter with the *Craven Herald* at Skipton we spoke regularly on the phone.

'That's how she met Daniel, her husband. He was a freelance photographer for them. I went up to see her a couple of times, but that became more difficult with my shifts, and then seven years ago, right out of the blue, she told me she was getting married and asked me to be her bridesmaid. It was a great weekend and we promised to keep in touch but you know how it is. This job is unforgiving at times.

'The last time I actually paid her a visit was the first Christmas after she got married. She invited me to go up and stay with her and Daniel for Boxing Day. I went up there for two nights and we caught up. She told me how happy she was, that Daniel was lovely, and that they were planning to start a family in a couple of years' time.' Alix paused for a moment, looking thoughtful. 'I'm trying to recall our conversations. It's such a long time ago now. We mainly talked about how our lives had changed since leaving uni. And she was interested in my job so I told her a few funny stories, as you do. That was it. If anything unusual was happening in her life, she never mentioned it. And when we spoke on the phone afterwards it was usually Elise quizzing me as to whether I was seeing anyone or not.'

'So, at no time did she mention receiving any unwanted phone calls or being followed?'

Alix thought about the question for a few seconds before answering. 'Not before she went missing, she didn't, but I've just remembered something from when we were at uni.'

'What was that?' Both Lauren and Hamlet said the same thing together and they acknowledged one another with a slight smile before returning their attention to Alix.

'She told me about a student on her course who was constantly following her around wherever she went. Even when she went out into town or to the pub, he'd be there. Not causing any nuisance or harassing her, nothing like that, just hanging around wanting to talk and be with her. She found it uncomfortable.' Alix lifted her eyes to the ceiling, deep in thought. Then she said, 'I remember now, she first mentioned this just before we broke up on our first summer hols. We were getting ready to go out into Sheffield and she asked me for some advice about a lad she was doing a work placement with who she felt was coming on a bit strong. She didn't fancy him and wanted to let him down gently, but was unsure how to go about it because she felt sorry for him.

'If I remember rightly, this lad had latched on to Elise after he'd told her about some difficult family circumstances. I don't remember the exact details but it was something to do with living with his gran because his parents had split up and he was finding it difficult coping because she had been diagnosed with cancer and was undergoing treatment and he was spending all his time looking after her and it was getting him down. Elise had experienced something similar with her gran and she told him about what support he could get and then helped him with a couple of phone calls.

'She told me that after that he was constantly seeking her out, and she said it was getting her down having to listen to him day after day moaning on about his life. I think she felt sorry for him because he repeatedly told how thankful he was to her for helping him, and kept asking if they could meet up one night. She was running out of excuses why she couldn't meet him and wanted my advice.

'I'm afraid I didn't help. I made a bit of a joke about her being such a soft touch. I told her he was just spinning her a yarn to get into her knickers and we ended up having a bit of a joke about excuses she could use to put him off. I asked her a couple of times if she had managed to fob him off and she said that he was starting to get creepy. I asked her in what way and she told me he'd started following her on social media and sending her emails about his feelings for her.

'I told her she needed to nip it in the bud and tell him quite simply she didn't fancy him, so she did, and he went off sick from uni. One day she came to my room in a bit of a state, telling me she'd spotted him a couple of times when she'd gone into town shopping and a couple of times when she'd used the tram. And she'd got some more emails from him to the effect that she'd led him on and that she was nothing but a heartless bitch. I told her she needed to report him to the principal, so she did. Just before the summer break she told me he'd left the course and she felt awful about it, but I told her it was for the best.'

'And did she hear from him again?' Lauren asked.

'Not that I'm aware of. She certainly never mentioned it. When we broke up, I went down to my mum and dad's place and she went home to Derbyshire. She came down to stay with me for a few weeks before we came back to uni and I asked her if she'd heard from him, but she said she'd not seen hide nor hair of him.'

Alix's voice trailed off and Hamlet realised she had reached the point where her own life had changed forever. It had been during that summer that she had been raped at her family's vicarage: something she had shared with him in a drunken moment. He could see from Alix's glazed look that her thoughts were suddenly there. *Back at that moment.*

Reacting quickly, to bring her mind back to the present, he said, 'Do you remember the name of this lad, the student?'

She shook her head and replied, 'No, sorry. It was almost ten years ago now and back then it felt like no big deal. Just a lad with a crush on my friend who needed to be told where to get off, and he did.' She paused then added, 'It shouldn't be too hard to find out though. Elise did report him, and the guy was suspended. So there should be a record of it.'

Hamlet nodded. 'You know I mentioned that offenders always make a mistake somewhere along the line? This could well be our killer, and this could well be the mistake he made.'

Later that afternoon, back in MIT, Hamlet finished watching a twenty-minute YouTube video on embalming presented by an American pathologist and shook his head as he closed down the programme. While not shocked, he was surprised that such a thing should be allowed on a social media platform and also just how easy it was to embalm someone.

The only medical knowledge anyone required was knowing where the carotid and femoral arteries were to insert the tubes to pump in the embalming solution and to drain out the blood. That was it. There was an issue with getting the requisite equipment and solutions to carry out the process but he knew one could get almost anything from the internet these days. It was just a matter of finding the companies who were willing to trade illegally, and there were plenty of those.

He made a note to follow up those lines of enquiry because he knew it certainly hadn't been an issue for their killer. Earlier, in the bunker, behind a closed door off the War Room, they had discovered the place where he had embalmed his five victims. As soon as the CSI officer had opened the door into the anteroom the stench had hit them all like a sledgehammer. It had reminded Hamlet of rancid meat, making him gag so much that he'd had to leave the bunker immediately for some fresh air.

It had been twenty minutes before he had been able to summon up the courage to return and when he had, he'd been greeted by the two forensic officers and Alix, the three of them wearing smug grins. By pinching his nose and breathing only shallowly through his mouth, he had been able to hold back the stink and watch with fascination as the two CSI officers processed the room. It contained an old metal bed covered with a stained mattress, and set around it three trestle tables holding an electrical pump, battery-powered generator and six plastic drums containing embalming solutions. It had reminded him of scenes he had seen on the news of crude operating theatres in war-torn countries.

He had stayed there, putting up with the smell for well over an hour, thinking about what type of person could have done this to those women, losing himself in his thoughts until Alix had dragged him back to the moment, saying that there was nothing more they could do, and making the decision to quit for the day and return back to the office to update the team.

He swore he could still smell the stench of stale blood on his clothes and couldn't wait to get out of them and climb into the shower. Putting aside his notes, he craned his head over the desk-divide, wanting to chat to Alix about the day's events and particularly to see if she was all right following the discovery that one of the killer's victims was once her friend at university, and was surprised to find she wasn't there.

Quickly scanning the room, he caught sight of her by the incident boards. She was Blu Tacking photographs she had taken on her phone of the crime scene in the bunker in preparation for the briefing, when the full facts of the days' find would be delivered to the team and the next stages of the investigation deliberated and proposed.

Hamlet checked his watch. Almost 5 p.m. The day had flown. They had finally quit from the bunker shortly after three. Six hours he had been there. While getting out of their forensic suits, the CSI supervisor had come over to them and said that they were also quitting for the day and that it was a mammoth task because of years of activity and use of the bunker. There were hundreds of fingerprints and lots of DNA, and reinforcements would be joining them tomorrow. It could still be several days of work before they finished harvesting the forensics because of the contamination and until then they would be leaving the bodies in situ.

It was at that point, conscious of press numbers, which had increased since their arrival, that Lauren called in additional uniform staff to maintain security of the bunker, briefing two officers appointed to the task before leaving. As they left, Hamlet hoped he wouldn't have to return tomorrow and endure another day of *that* smell.

Alix had just finished posting up the last of the photographs and begun adding information to the chronicle of events when Lauren entered the room, making her way to the front. She exchanged a quick word with Alix who put down the marker pen and returned to her desk.

Lauren studied the murder board and then turned to face her team. 'Okay, briefing everyone.' She watched them put their mobiles on silent and get themselves comfortable before continuing. 'As you all know, in the early hours of this morning a group of three bunker enthusiasts broke into an MOD bunker situated in a field at Low Bradfield, and after a cursory search of the place entered the War Room where they found Hayley Stevenson and five dead females in a bizarre setting that you can all see for yourselves up on the board.' She thumbed back over her shoulder to the collection of shocking photos. 'Uniform and CID from Stocksbridge were first on scene and, finding Hayley was still alive, called for an ambulance.

'She was rushed to the Hallamshire where she was diagnosed as suffering from severe dehydration and malnutrition. I was informed just before five this morning and turned out. We didn't realise at first that the bodies you see behind me were actually real people. We all thought they were mannequins and you can see why from these pictures.

'The discovery of Hayley was my prime focus, but once it was brought to my attention the bodies weren't dummies I called out CSI, task force and Alix, Nate and Hamlet to join me. They have spent most of the day at the scene but have had to call it a day because of the sheer amount of work still ahead.

'Both CSI and task force will be returning tomorrow when search parameters will be increased around the bunker and a full forensic team will be working inside it. A decision has been made to leave the bodies in situ until their job is done and so the bunker is off-limits until they finish.

'I want to first address the finding of Hayley.' She pointed to a blown-up copy of one of the photos. Hayley wasn't in the shot but it showed the stained mattress against the corner of the room upon which she had been discovered. The wall behind the mattress looked to be bloodstained. It had a chain fastened to it, the links trailing down to the mattress. Beside the mattress two empty plastic litre water bottles, a couple of empty sandwich packets and a screwed-up large crisp packet could be seen.

Lauren tapped the image. 'Hayley was found lying on this mattress. The chain you can see dangling from the wall had a metal neck brace attached to it. That had been fastened around her neck and padlocked. She had to be bolt-cropped from it before they could put her in the ambulance. The sandwich packets, empty crisp packet and empty water bottles have been the only food and water source we have found so it's no wonder the state she was in if that's all she's had to eat and drink since she disappeared ten days ago.' Lauren's expression was grim. 'I'm hopeful that once she comes round, she'll be able to recognise who abducted her so we can put him away for the rest of his natural.

'On that note, Hayley is making good progress and is expected to make a full physical recovery. She is still on a drip and is very weak but Katie has said that she's opened her eyes briefly and asked what has happened to her, but that's all she's said so far. She is still very drowsy. However, the consultant has said that if she carries on making the progress she has, we should be able to speak with her tomorrow.'

'Now to our victims.' Lauren started by introducing Elise Farmer, formally Lewis, who was 24 when she disappeared five years ago, recounting the story Alix had told her about the day she vanished. The tasks she wrote up on the board beneath Elise's name was to find out who that student was who had been suspended and request a copy of her missing report.

Next, she presented Molly Fraser, the young woman who disappeared after losing control of her car in the snow, crashing it into a wall only a few miles from the bunker. She had vanished four years ago. Following her came Sophie Booker, the student from Rotherham, who disappeared from a pub car park whilst out drinking with friends. Then Madison Yates, who disappeared while on her way home from a party.

Finally, she came to Jessica McKenna, who was last seen eighteen months ago getting off the Supertram at Cricket Inn Road, just a short walk from her home, but sadly never arrived.

'Five young women who were just starting out their lives, taken off the streets by someone…' Lauren banged a hand over one of the photographs of the embalmed women. 'And while we don't yet know how he killed them, we know from finding Hayley that more than likely they would have been chained up like an animal before they died. And for that reason alone, we owe it to them to make sure we catch this man before he gets a chance to take anyone else. Hopefully tomorrow Hayley Stevenson will be able to identify him.'

'If she's unable to, he won't stop,' Hamlet said softly.

Every head in the room spun around.

Lauren stared at him for a moment before saying, 'Why do you say that, Hamlet?'

He eased himself forward. 'Our perpetrator has been given the moniker "The Wedding Killer", and at first it was by way of a joke, but given what we've seen today it's certainly apt. Our man clearly has a fantasy about a certain type of woman he wants to be with. At the moment all I can see is a physical resemblance between the victims, though I'm sure there is more substance than that, certainly in the killer's mind. What I do see is that he has a fantasy about marrying them, the wedding dresses put on all the victims is evidence of that. And if he can't have his bride alive, accepting her place beside him, then he'll have her in death. The line from the classical wedding vows painted above the makeshift altar is reinforcement of that. Losing Hayley will not deter him from his fantasy. He has to find a new bride. For all we know he may already have his next victim lined up.'

It was just after seven p.m. when Hamlet pulled up outside his cabin. Most of his colleagues had headed off to the pub from work, and although he'd been invited to join them, he'd politely declined, informing them that it had been almost twelve hours since he'd last seen Lucky, and journeyed home instead.

The moment he opened the French doors Lucky was by his legs, sniffing and wanting a fuss. Hamlet bent down and ruffled the little dog's back, receiving lots of greeting licks to his neck and chin in return. 'Been bored, boy?' he said, tossing his car keys onto the coffee table. 'Ready for a walk, are we?'

he added, loosening his tie and rolling it around his hand before dropping the bundle beside his keys.

Lucky's head was up, his brown eyes imploring. Hamlet laughed. 'Simple things in life, eh?' He untied his laces, pulled off his brogues and slipped on his walking shoes, all the time being scrutinised by Lucky.

The moment Hamlet stepped through the doors onto the veranda Lucky flashed past his legs, scampered down the steps and shot away to the nearest tree to cock his leg. Hamlet headed toward the stream, taking a meandering path to the edge of the woods and then diverted off to the Neolithic burial chamber before heading back to the cabin.

He took the journey at a steady pace, thinking over the events of the day. A lot was tumbling around inside his head, most of it in the form of flashbacks of the bodies inside the bunker, yet there had been moments when he had been morbidly fascinated by the crime scene.

He also couldn't stop thinking about Alix. After years of wondering what had happened to her friend Elise, she had been the first to find her body and learn how she had met her gruesome end. *That can't have been easy.* She'd been unusually quiet. When they had travelled back to work and he'd asked her if she wanted to talk about it, she'd snapped back, 'I'm fine', and they had driven back in virtual silence, her knuckles white where she gripped the steering wheel. As he neared the cabin, he made a mental note to ring her later and check how she was, even if she didn't want to talk.

Dusk was approaching and the temperature had dropped. Even inside the cabin it was cool, and he put a match to the fire, watching the logs in the grate spark as flames engulfed them, before making his way into the kitchen.

He was starving and he guessed Lucky would be too. He gave the terrier a mix of wet food and dry kibble and then went to the fridge to see what there was for him. He saw a pack of bacon that hadn't yet been opened, and there were some mushrooms that were just starting to turn, so he took them out, added two eggs, together with two slices of dry bread from the cupboard and began cooking an all-day breakfast.

As he prepared the meal something was gnawing at the back of his thoughts. It was to do with Alix and Elise. Something that had been said. He tried to think back on the various conversations they'd had, but there had been such a jumble of disparate things discussed that he couldn't hone in on any particular aspect of the exchanges. He would have to give Alix a call. Use the excuse of checking if she was okay to see if it would trigger anything.

It was almost 9 p.m. by the time he finished his meal. He washed and cleared away his dishes and then put on the news to see if there was anything about the day's discovery. He expected there to be because he had seen the press presence at Low Bradfield treble in size over the day, and before leaving work he had heard that camera crews had also besieged the hospital where Hayley had been admitted.

He didn't have to wait long. The investigation was the first item. The report started with a close-up on officers searching the fields in front of the bunker. After a few seconds the shot panned back slowly, its focus centring upon the news reporter. The camera framed her blonde head and shoulders and she began to speak.

'Police investigating the disappearance of Sheffield student Hayley Stevenson ten days ago are today searching an old World War Two bunker in the Peak District where the missing 21-year-old was discovered in the early hours of this morning.

She is currently in hospital undergoing treatment where detectives are waiting to interview her.

'We also understand that police have also discovered five bodies in the bunker, all believed to be female, although South Yorkshire Police are yet to confirm this. This afternoon I spoke with farmer George Hemming whose land the bunker is on.'

A clip was then shown of a man, who looked to be in his sixties, wearing a flat cap and checked shirt, a rambling stone barn in the background. He said that officers had visited him early that morning and told him they had found a woman unconscious in the bunker and asked if he had seen anything suspicious.

The clip ended and the news journalist ended her report by saying, 'While police have confirmed it is Hayley that was found unconscious in the bunker behind me, they are not yet giving out any details about the bodies they have found.'

Short and sweet, Hamlet thought to himself as he turned down the volume. He knew that would change from tomorrow. They had released the three bunker enthusiasts late that afternoon and he was sure they would want to get in on the act; after all, it would increase their YouTube viewings no end. They would also want a comment from the family and the police. It isn't every day that the bodies of five young women are found in an old bunker, and once they learn that each one had been embalmed, which no doubt they would, they were going to have a field day.

The police were going to come under pressure to make an arrest, and pretty quickly from his experience. He remembered what had happened to him after they discovered Helen and his parents murdered.

They had been under pressure then and locked him up for six months before releasing him, realising they had got the wrong man. He was going to do his damnedest to make sure they got the right person for this and not make an innocent man suffer.

He mused on that for a good couple of minutes and then he decided it was time to ring Alix. He would use the news feature as a ruse to get around to asking her how she was. He rang her mobile and she picked it up after three rings.

'Hi Hamlet.'

'I'm just ringing to see if you've watched the news. I've just seen it.'

'I saw it in the pub with the others. Lauren got a phone call from the chief after it ended. He wants her to do a news conference tomorrow. She's gone to meet with the communications team.'

Hamlet thought her words sounded slurred. He said, 'You sound as though you've had a good time. Did I miss much?'

'Not really. Nate got a bit arsey after Lauren left. I ended up having words with him.'

'About me?'

'And he had a dig about me. I ended up telling him to fuck off and left.'

Hamlet let out a short laugh. 'Not like you.'

'He can be a tit sometimes. I opened a bottle of wine when I got home, which I'll regret in the morning.' Breaking off, she continued, 'Did you want me for anything special?'

'Only to see if you'd seen the news … and to see how you are? Today must have been a real shock for you.'

There was no response, instead he caught what he thought was Alix stifling a sob. He asked, 'Are you okay?'

'You know I'm not,' she snapped, 'so why do you ask?'

He responded tentatively, 'I'm sorry to pry, Alix. I guessed that in the car when we left the bunker, that's why I didn't push you. I just want to let you know I'm here for you, if you want to talk?' He heard her swallowing hard. It sounded like she was suppressing another sob. He left it a moment and then said, 'You know where I am if you need me. I'm a good listener, you know that.'

Several beats of silence passed between them and then Alix said, 'I'm sorry I snapped at you like that, Hamlet. I know you only mean the best for me. If I'd have opened up this afternoon, I'd have been in no fit state when I got back to work and I knew I needed to be.'

'I get that, Alix. No problem.'

After a few seconds, she said, 'I've just got off the phone to Elise's mum. We've had a cry together. I told her I couldn't tell her what had happened to Elise, and I apologised for that, but I was able to tell her what we would be doing regarding the investigation. I think she understood. I felt awful not being able to tell her much.'

'I'm sure she'll understand.'

'Anyway, I've promised to keep in touch. And I've promised to go up and see them once I can get away. I made a promise that we'd do everything we can to catch whoever harmed Elise. I just hope I can keep it.'

'We will, Alix,' he replied softly. 'We will.' He wanted to talk longer, particularly to go back over some of the things she had mentioned about her and Elise when they were at university, to end that niggling in his brain, but he knew now was not the right time. Instead, he said, 'Elise's mum will have appreciated your call. Although you couldn't say too much, you'll have reassured her that we're going to do everything we can to catch her daughter's killer. She'll be comforted by that.'

'Thank you, Hamlet. You're a kind man, you know that?'

'You're drunk, Alix,' he said, laughing.

She returned a laugh. 'I'll see you tomorrow morning.'

THIRTEEN

Hamlet was up at first light. He'd had a restless night, and still hadn't managed to resolve the niggle in his brain. He hoped the morning briefing would prompt something, and if it didn't, he'd go over it with Alix as soon as they got a quiet moment together.

Flinging open the French doors to let out Lucky, he was greeted by intense sunlight piercing through the woodland canopy, smothering the fauna in warm sunshine. Even the veranda radiated warmth and it wasn't yet 6.30 a.m. It instantly refreshed him, motivating him to go in early and he took Lucky on an invigorating though shorter than normal walk.

Upon their return, checking the weather forecast for the day and seeing it was going to reach highs of 76 degrees, Hamlet left one of the French doors open a fraction, set out full bowls of food and water on the veranda and set off for work. On his way he called in at a convenience store and grabbed a copy of each of the local newspapers to check out what had been reported about yesterday's discovery.

He got in shortly after seven, made his way to the canteen, ordered poached eggs on toast and a mug of tea and sat down to read the first of the papers. The moment he caught sight of the photograph beside the article on the front page of the *Sheffield Telegraph*, his guts started to churn.

The picture showed Hayley curled up unconscious on the stained mattress, the chain still around her neck. The writer of the piece was none other than Crime Correspondent Matt Ross, the same journalist who had controversially brought the police press conference for Hayley to an abrupt end with his knowledge about her being a dancer.

Now in print, he was causing more damage to the investigation. Hayley's parents would be mortified once they saw this and would immediately blame the investigation team for it, even though he was already reading in the second paragraph it had come courtesy of one of the bunker enthusiasts.

Damn! He had thought Nate Fox had seized all the enthusiast's mobiles containing the footage of their night-time adventure, but this picture clearly proved he hadn't. One of them had obviously secreted his phone and managed to keep it hidden. Now he had sold the picture together with his story. He wondered if they had got pictures of the bodies and was negotiating to sell those?

This was a disaster. Hamlet read on to see what other damage had been inflicted upon the investigation.

Hayley Stevenson was last seen outside a busy Sheffield pub, close to the student bar she had just left, after which she mysteriously vanished, leaving behind her mobile and driving licence. Yesterday she was found by three men trussed up inside a World War II bunker in a quiet rural hamlet on the outskirts of Sheffield. She is currently in hospital helping the police identify the man who abducted her. Five other bodies were found in the same bunker and are all believed to be women who disappeared from the Sheffield area over the past few years. Police are not commenting but young women from the University are calling on the police for added protection. Continued on page 4.

Hamlet whipped over two pages where another headline stated, *I was targeted on the same night Hayley Stevenson went missing.* There was a close-up picture of a young blonde woman, the caption beneath it reading *19-year-old Summer Wheelhouse was the victim of a sexual attack hours before Hayley went missing.*

Hamlet had just started to read on further when a voice disturbed him.

'Thought I'd find you here.'

He looked up to see Alix walking over to him. Behind her was Nate Fox.

She dipped her head backwards, saying, 'I bumped into this reprobate in the car park,' and joined him at the table. Nate pulled up another chair and sat down beside her.

Hamlet turned the newspaper the right way up for them to see and said, 'Just reading the *Telegraph*. Have you seen this article?'

'I haven't seen the paper but it's all over the news this morning. Caught it on the radio on the way in. They've got a picture of Hayley, apparently.'

Hamlet folded back the paper to the front page. He jabbed at the picture of Hayley curled up on the mattress. 'This one?' he said.

'Fuck!' Alix exclaimed. 'How the hell did they get that?'

Hamlet stared at Nate. He said, 'One of the enthusiasts, according to the report.'

Alix shot a glance at Nate. 'I thought you'd seized all their phones?'

Nate immediately looked put out. He snapped back, 'I did. We took all their clothing as well for forensics. One of them must have shoved their phone up their arse. How was I to know that? You can't blame me for this.'

Alix was about to respond when Hamlet intervened, 'He's right, Alix. You can't blame Nate over this. Those enthusiasts weren't suspects as such. They didn't warrant being searched intrusively like that.'

126

Alix looked from Nate to Hamlet and then back to Nate. 'I apologise for that, Nate. Hamlet's right, you're not to blame.'

Nate scraped back his chair and stormed out of the canteen.

Lauren opened the briefing by venting her frustration at the latest gratuitous media publicity, explaining that she had just returned from a breakfast meeting with a not-too-happy Chief Constable who was demanding to know who had leaked the photo of Hayley to the press. She stopped, staring into the audience, tapping her foot as she waited for a response.

Nate nervously cleared his throat and gave an account as to how he believed one of the bunker enthusiasts had managed to secrete away the evidence while in custody, after which she let out a lengthy sigh of irritation and said, 'Well at least that gives me some ammunition to fire back at the command team. No one would foresee someone going to those lengths just to retain some photos. I hope he got piles retrieving it.'

Many of the team sniggered. Lauren then told them that the Media Communications team had been inundated with requests for interviews, saying the discovery had attracted international interest and she had agreed to a press conference that afternoon to satiate their appetite. She would be speaking with the victim's families that morning to prepare them for press intrusion and also appointing a family liaison officer to each one. She would also be apologising to Hayley's parents for the mistake, and in support of Nate, added, 'Although I don't know what else could have been done to prevent this. It's just one of those unfortunate things that we have to hold our hands up to.'

DC Nick Lewis raised the issue about the reported attack on Summer Wheelhouse, referring to the article in the *Telegraph*.

Lauren responded, 'Just before I came in to briefing, I managed to track down the officer who dealt with her. The attack on her was a grope by a drunken young man on West Street as she was leaving the pub. The officer tells me he has CCTV evidence capturing a man in his twenties, worse the wear for drink, who pinched her bottom just as she was coming out of the pub and he was going in. The officer has not yet managed to trace the man who carried out the assault and I have asked for a copy of the footage to be sent to me so we can look into it. Whilst it is no doubt a very uncomfortable moment that has left a lasting impression on Summer, it does not appear to bear any similarity to what happened to Hayley.

'On that note, a "Safe on the Streets" group has been formed by students from the university who are already lobbying local MP's that Sheffield is not a safe place for women. The chief has told me he has already been informed there will be a gathering outside the university tonight whose numbers will be bussed across to Low Bradfield for an evening vigil near the bunker. It is not expected to be a violent protest but resources will be deployed there just in case.

'The demonstration will be videoed, but I want you, Nate, and Katie to attend and see if you recognise anyone who might warrant a visit later to see what they were doing there.' Receiving a nod of acknowledgment from them she continued, 'The vigil means we are bringing things forward with regards removal of the bodies. Forensics will have finished in the War Room around lunchtime so we are gearing everything up for that time to take them out of there and get them to the Medico-Legal Centre. Their post-mortems have been arranged for tomorrow, which will give us an indication of how they all died.'

Looking to Alix, she said, 'I'd like you to go to that, and take along Hamlet for experience. And while I've got you, I also want you and Hamlet to go and interview Hayley at the hospital. I have been informed that she is well enough to talk. See if she can identify the man who took her. We could really do with a breakthrough on this.'

FOURTEEN

Before leaving for the Hallamshire, Alix put in a phone call to the hospital and after a chat with a nurse on ITU learned that Hayley's condition had improved. The nurse asked Hayley if she was comfortable with Hamlet attending and Hayley said it was OK. Scribbling down the details Alix grabbed her jacket, gave Hamlet the nod and made her way down to her car.

The journey through Sheffield was tediously slow as per usual with side roads around the teaching hospital either 'residents only parking' or painted up with double yellow lines. Eventually they found a spot a good half mile away and walked back.

Hayley was in a ward on the third floor and they rode up in the lift. At the ward station Alix caught the attention of the nurse practitioner, and after a quick chat she was pointed along the corridor to a side room where a police officer was sat outside, head down, eyes scrolling through her phone. The young officer's head snapped up as Alix and Hamlet approached, a look of guilt on her face as she quickly lowered her phone, hiding the screen.

Probably on Facebook, Alix thought, greeting the young officer with a smile to put her mind at ease that she wasn't in trouble. 'Bored?' she said, showing her ID.

The officer looked at it, popped her phone into her bag and entered Alix's details on her clipboard. 'Just a bit. I've been here since six,' she replied.

'Not had a break?'

'My relief's not due until eleven.'

'Anybody in with her?' Alix asked, doffing her head at the door.

'Not at the moment. The nurses have been in and she's had breakfast.'

'Parents?'

'They came last night, according to the log. Left shortly after eight. End of visiting time.'

'Okay. Look, if you want to nip off and get a bite to eat, we're going to be here talking with Hayley for at least an hour.'

The officer gave Alix a hesitant look.

Alix said, 'I'll take the responsibility. We're the only ones who should be seeing her today. If you're uncomfortable leaving us, no problem. But if you at least want to grab a toilet break and a drink then we'll be in with her until you get back.'

'I'd appreciate a quick break, thanks.' The officer rose from her seat, gathered up her bag and trotted away.

Hayley was propped up, resting on a bank of pillows when Alix and Hamlet entered the room. She flicked open her eyes as they closed the door behind them. It looked as if she had been dozing.

Alix introduced them both, pushing a high-back chair towards her bed, and told her they had come to talk about what happened to her. Hayley immediately pushed herself back against her pillows, her posture rigid, fear registering in her eyes. Alix spoke gently. 'Hayley, I can't imagine for one minute what you have gone through, and we don't want to cause you any more anguish than you've already suffered, but we really need to speak to you about what happened. Do you feel up to talking to us? If would be really helpful if you can.'

Hayley slowly nodded an assent.

'Thank you, Hayley.' Alix made herself comfortable in the chair. Hamlet pulled up another chair.

Alix activated the recording app on her phone and set it down on the bed. 'Before we talk about the night when you were taken, Hayley, I'd first like to ask you about the mysterious phone calls you received. From the enquiries we've made since you were taken, we believe those could be the start of everything that has happened to you and I want to take you back to them. Can you remember when those calls started and what was said at all?'

Hayley raised her eyes to the ceiling for a brief moment before returning her gaze to Alix. 'I remember them very well because they were so weird. The first call was about five weeks before I was grabbed. I remember that because I'd just got the job at Pink Rhino's and I was waiting to talk to the woman who would be sorting out my first shift there. I was at the gym and it came up as unknown caller. I answered it and it was a man's voice who said "Hayley," and believing it was someone from the club I answered "Yes," and then he said something to the effect of, "You don't know me, but I know you. A lot about you in fact, and I'm a big admirer. I'd like to get to know you more, would you like that?" I asked who it was and he just said, "As I just said, an admirer."

'The call really rattled me and I ended the call. Half an hour later, I'd just got out of the shower and was getting dressed and the same unknown caller came up. I asked him who he was, and he said something like, "I've already told you, an admirer." Then he said, "That wasn't very nice hanging up. I only want to get to know you better. I'd like to meet you."

'That call really unnerved me because of the way he spoke. There was no emotion to his voice. It was almost as if he was reading from a script. I told him I already had a boyfriend, which I hadn't. I tried to be kind. I didn't want to upset him, and that's when he said, "I know you don't have a boyfriend, Hayley. As I've already said, I know a lot about you."

'When he said that it really freaked me out, and I told him I wasn't interested in ever meeting him and if he rang me again, I'd report him to the police. Then I hung up and blocked his number.

'I told my friend, Sarah, about it. Sarah helped me get the job at the club. She's also a pole-dancer there. We both used to do gymnastics together. That's how I came to apply. She told me there was a knack to it but because of the gymnastics training it would be a doddle for me and the money was good. Better than working behind a bar, which was what I was doing at weekends. She got me the interview and went with me. I was nervous about going there, I can tell you, but the manager was really nice, not sleazy at all, and he fixed it up for me to go and do a trial, which was easier than I expected, and the manager said I'd get a call from his deputy to sort out my shifts.'

'We've spoken with the manager Harry Malvern, and we know you've been working there for a few months,' Alix said.

Hayley nodded, her eyes suddenly welling up with tears. Her bottom lip started quivering. 'I didn't tell my mum and dad because I knew they wouldn't approve. And I didn't tell my sister, Becca, either. Sarah was the only person who knew about me working there. You know what some people think about those places. I found out last night that they knew about it when they came to visit me. They said they were told when they did a press conference after I'd gone missing, but they've been really good about it, even though I'm embarrassed.'

'You shouldn't be, Hayley. It's a job. You've not done anything wrong.'

'I know, but it's what everyone at uni's going to know me for now.'

'Hayley, do you mind me asking a few questions?' Hamlet interjected.

She switched her gaze to him.

'The man who phoned you. You said he talked as if he was reading from a script. What did you mean by that comment?'

'Just that it didn't sound as if he was talking naturally. It was slow. As if he was reading the words.'

'Do you think he could have been disguising his voice?'

She shrugged her shoulders. 'Possibly.'

'Any accent or dialect?'

'No. Though now you've mentioned it, I did get the impression he was local, or at least from Yorkshire.'

Hamlet nodded. 'And how many times did you hear him speak?'

'Three more times after those first two calls. The next call came roughly a week after. He rang on another number that came up as unknown caller. As soon as he started to talk I ended the call and blocked the number. I did get another two calls from another unknown number but I ended them and blocked those as well.'

'And during those other three calls, did he say anything?'

'Sort of. The third call he said that it wasn't nice of me to hang up and block his calls. All he wanted to do was get to know me better. Our Becca was with me on that occasion and I ended it, telling him to leave me alone. I think I called him a weirdo.'

'Yes, we've spoken to your sister. She told us about the calls.' Alix picked the conversation back up again. 'And we also know about the anonymous wedding invitation you received. We recovered it from your waste bin. You'd torn it up.'

'That came in the post the day before he took me.'

'How do you know it was from the same person?'

'Because he told me when I got in his car. I thought it was the taxi I'd ordered. I realised it wasn't when I didn't see the meter inside, but it was too late by then. He said, "You've not responded to my invitation, Hayley." And that's when he zapped me.'

'Zapped you?' Alix and Hamlet responded at the same time.

'I think it was one of those taser things. I just remember seeing blue flashes as he turned round and pushed it into my chest. That's all I remember. There was a sharp pain and then the next thing I woke up in the dark.'

'In the bunker,' Alix responded.

'Bunker?'

'Yes. We found you in an old war bunker. You were unconscious.'

'I didn't know that. Mum and dad haven't said anything about where I was found. I thought I was in a cellar underground. It was so dark. I couldn't see anything. Mum and dad told me last night I was found with some dead women who'd also been missing. It has been on the news and in the papers.'

Alix nodded. 'That's right, Hayley. Didn't you see them?'

'I never saw anything. It was so dark. I smelt something but I thought it might have been a dead animal. A cat or a rat or something. I had no idea it was dead bodies.' She shuddered. 'I'm glad now I couldn't see anything. I don't know how I would have reacted.' After a short pause she said, 'How did the women die? Is it the same man who took me that killed them?'

'We don't know how they died yet. We have a forensic team still at the bunker and there will be post-mortems on the other victims. We think the same person that took you also killed those women.'

'Oh God. I'm so lucky. Mum and dad say that the news said it's five women you've found?'

'That's right.'

'Do I know any of them?'

'We don't think so. We're not releasing the names until we've spoken with the families properly. Once we do release their names, we will talk to you about them. See if you know any of them. You were missing for eleven days, but they had all been missing for much longer.'

Hayley looked shocked. 'And you've locked the man up who's done all this?'

Alix pursed her lips. 'Not yet. That's why we're talking to you. You were found by three men who broke into the place because they thought it was an empty bunker. As soon as they found you, they called us.' She wasn't going to mention that it was one of those shits who had sold the image of her to the media. She would deal with that if the question came.

Before Alix could ask another question Hamlet interjected, 'Hayley, when Alix said you had been missing for eleven days, you looked shocked.'

'That's because I didn't know it had been that long. I can't remember much about my time there. I can't even remember at what stage I became unconscious. I think I might have been drugged, and it was so dark. I didn't know if it was day or night. It's been awful. I'm so lucky they found me.'

'What's the first thing you can recall?' Hamlet pressed.

'After I was zapped by the taser thing in the car, you mean?'

Hamlet nodded.

'Waking up and feeling this metal clamp around my neck, and realising that I was chained to the wall. I know I was on a mattress because I felt around me. I found some sandwiches on the bed, and a bag of crisps, and there were two big bottles of water that I had.' She paused and said, 'I think it was the water that was drugged. After I'd drunk some I started feeling drowsy and then I think I must have conked out. When I woke up, I had the most horrendous headache and my throat was so dry. I tried to avoid drinking any more but I got really thirsty so I just took a massive drink again. I thought even if it was drugged, at least I would be alive.

'After about half an hour after drinking again, I got to feeling sleepy and zonked out. That happened to me four times, and each time I woke up with a splitting headache. At least I'm alive.' Tears started to well up. Hamlet knew their time was short.

'When we found you, you were wearing jogging pants and a sweat top, not the clothing you were wearing when you went missing. Did you get changed into those?' Alix asked.

Hayley gave them a surprised look. 'No, I never got changed. He must have done that when I was unconscious. Probably when I was drugged.' She paused, then burst out crying. 'I can't remember. I can't remember,' she sobbed.

Alix reached over and gave her hand a comforting squeeze. 'Don't worry, Hayley. You're safe now. That's the main thing. He can't hurt you again.'

'And you've no idea who did this to me?'

'Not yet we don't, but we're hoping forensics are going to help us catch him.'

Hamlet asked, 'When you got into the car, you said you realised it wasn't a taxi because it didn't have a meter. Do you recall anything else about the car?'

She wiped away the tears with the back of her hand, closed her eyes for a few seconds and then opened them, answering, 'It was a dark colour and one with a boot. I think it was a BMW. I remember seeing the badge on the boot.'

Hamlet said, 'What about the seats? Leather? Fabric?'

'Fabric. Definitely fabric.'

'Anything else about the inside that you remember?'

'He had an air freshener of some sort dangling from the mirror. At least I think it was an air freshener. It was yellow. I can remember seeing it with the street lights.'

'You're doing really well, Hayley. This is a big help, believe me. And I've just one more question about the man who abducted you. Before he tasered you, did you get a look at him?'

'He was white. And he didn't look that old. Maybe mid to late twenties. And he was clean shaven.'

'What about hair?'

'I didn't see his hair. He was wearing a dark beanie type hat. It was pulled over his ears and covered his forehead.'

'Eyes? Did you notice those?'

'Dark,' Hayley responded, her voice breaking off momentarily. After a few seconds she said, 'I couldn't see them properly because I remember now that no interior light came on when I opened the door to get in. He had on a dark jumper as well. Could have been a sweatshirt. He turned round so fast and said, "You're mine, Hayley," and that's when I saw the taser in his hand.' Her bottom lip started trembling and more tears rolled down her cheeks.

'Hayley, I've just one more question to ask you and then we're done for the day,' Alix said. 'You said earlier that you were at the gym when you received the first call from the man. What gym was that?'

'Ponds Forge. Most of the students go there because of the discount.'

Alix glanced at Hamlet.

FIFTEEN

'One of the things I have been looking at is patterns the killer is adhering to that might make it easier to catch him,' Hamlet said at the evening briefing. He had already fed in what he and Alix had gained from speaking with Hayley earlier.

'Before the bodies of Elise, Molly, Sophie, Madison and Jessica were discovered by the bunker enthusiasts I had already noticed similarities in the appearance of the women who had gone missing, and therefore deduced that the abductor had a target type. I also learned that prior to them going missing each of them received a series of calls from unregistered pay-as-you-go numbers, and certainly two of them had also received identical wedding invitations.

'All of them, with the exception of Elise, were students at Sheffield University at the time of them going missing. In Elise's case she had been a student there but had since graduated and taken up a job as a reporter for a local newspaper in North Yorkshire when she disappeared.

'However, we know that Elise received unwarranted attention from a fellow male student at Sheffield uni and had reported him. Finding out who that person is is crucial, as he could be our man.

'Finally, interviewing Hayley has brought up another interesting link. Both she and Jessica were members of Ponds Forge gym at the time of going missing. What I have deduced from all of this is that he's organised. Highly organised. He learns about the women before he takes them. And we know that because he said as much to Hayley. He also works out the best time to strike.'

'So, are you able to give us any pointers about the man we're looking for?' Lauren asked. 'Do you have any views on the type of person he might be? Where he might live? What he does for a living?'

'I'm not a profiler. That's a different skill set. Everything I've just said is based on what I've learned from training with case notes and from my experience of dealing with patients in my previous job. What I will say is that I think he is single, because of the time he is able to spend following his victims, and also he has time to visit the bunker.'

Hamlet finished his input and Lauren took back the briefing. She told the team that the investigation was picking up pace. The forensics team had discovered a bathroom in the bunker where it appeared that the killer had soaked his 'brides' in a mixture of water and bleach to eradicate any trace of his DNA, and although he had taken the utmost care not to leave behind any forensic trace it appeared he may have slipped up because several bleach bottles had been discovered that carried fingerprints.

'I'm keeping my fingers crossed they belong to the killer, and the person who sold them,' she said, with a hopeful smile. She went on to tell them that the five bodies had all been ferried in private ambulances across to the Medico-Legal Centre, and a separate CSI team had been assigned to examine and swab down the corpses just in case the killer had missed areas when he had cleaned them.

'It's a long shot, but again I am hopeful,' she said. Pausing, she continued, 'The next stage are the post-mortems to determine how they were killed before they were embalmed. That's now been delayed until tomorrow to allow for a full forensic examination of each of the bodies. I anticipate that the post-mortems will take up most of the day tomorrow.

'It's been another busy day, and while Hayley hasn't been able to identify the person who abducted her, we now know that he tasered his victims to subdue them before transporting them to the bunker. We also know, thanks to Hayley, that he more than likely chained up his victims before he killed them. We also have to consider, given that Elise was taken five years ago, that he may have kept each victim alive for some period of time before he killed them.

'Alix and Hamlet are going to visit with Hayley once she's back at home in more relaxing surroundings and maybe she might just remember a little more that will help us catch him. And on that front, we are still waiting for the university to come back to us with regards the male student who harassed Elise when they were at uni together. Once we get a name, we can bring him in.

'On a final note, this afternoon's press conference was not one I want to rush into again. The case has created international interest. There must have been sixty reporters there and all of them clambering for a story. Whilst we have yet to formally confirm who the dead women are, they have already guessed four of them. Elise's name is the only one they haven't mentioned, but I'm sure it won't be long.

'Take it from me it is going to get very uncomfortable for a while and we are certainly going to be under intense scrutiny, so every time you leave this building you display the utmost professionalism. We need to present the right image no matter how bad things get. No unguarded comments please if you get ambushed.

'Mr and Mrs Stevenson have already been targeted, and so we have fixed up for them to go and stay with relatives near York for a few days, and once Hayley is discharged, we will be smuggling her out of the hospital to the same place.

'The media have also latched on to the wider concerns of the "Safe on the Streets" group and they will be joining them on tonight's vigil. I wouldn't be surprised to see our local MP's showing their faces, too.

'The chief has organised for a task force to be deployed together with the intelligence unit to video the crowds. So, on that note, Nate and Katie, you do not need to go to Low Bradfield this evening. You can have an early finish with the rest of the team. The pub beckons.'

The Sheaf Quay pub was busy with city centre blue-collar workers who had not yet wended their way home and the atmosphere inside was lively. The MIT team had taken up a corner of the bar.

Hamlet drank his beer listening in on different conversions, taking in the enthusiasm with which they shared their snippets, reminding him of war stories he had shared with former colleagues when he had been a newly qualified doctor in A&E.

He finished his beer, savouring every mouthful, and was tempted to have another but he had to get back to Lucky, and not wishing to be a party-pooper, being the first to leave, he opted for a small coke which would give him another half hour before he disappeared.

He could already see some were well into their second drink and he guessed that after another one they wouldn't notice him go. Before going, he was determined to take Alix to one side and see if he could have a private chat with her. He particularly wanted to quiz her about Elise, get some background about their time at uni together.

He saw she had just finished her wine, and he leaned in to her ear and said quietly, 'I'll get these, I'm only having a coke and then I need to get off for Lucky.' She gave him a look that told him she understood and handed over her empty glass. He said, 'Can I have a chat with you?'

She offered him a puzzled look. 'Something up? Nate giving you a hard time again?'

'No. Nothing's wrong. I just want a quiet word, that's all. Can we go outside when I get these? It'll only take ten minutes.'

'Sure.'

He bought the drinks and led her outside, which was bathed in strong evening sunlight. The outside seating area faced the canal basin, where a dozen or so narrowboats were moored on still water. It was a tranquil setting and a lot of the end of day workers had gravitated here, filling most of the picnic tables overlooking the canal. Hamlet spotted an empty bench and plonked himself down, Alix sitting opposite.

'What's so important?'

'I've been wanting to ask you some questions about Elise but not been able to get the right moment.'

She let out a soft sigh. 'Is that all? I thought something serious had happened.'

'I didn't want anyone eavesdropping in on what I want to ask you. It's a little bit sensitive. I saw the way you reacted when you mentioned that Elise had come down to your parent's vicarage during the summer. I wasn't sure if Lauren knew about what had happened to you.'

Alix took a long drink of her wine and said, 'You're right, Hamlet. I've never told Lauren about what happened to me. You, my counsellor, the police at Cambridgeshire and Elise are the only ones who know about that. I wish I hadn't told you now. Too much to drink that night.'

'It wasn't just the drink. It was the right moment. You needed to talk about it.'

Her mouth tightened momentarily, then her face relaxed. 'Yes, you're right. I did need to talk about it. You caught me at a vulnerable moment.'

'Are you able to talk about it now, because I have some burning questions that have been building up inside me since we found Elise and I think it might help the investigation. They came to me during briefing.'

Alix looked around her, checking no one was in earshot even though they were talking quietly. 'What do you want to ask?'

'It was something you said after you recognised Elise in the bunker and ran outside. You talked about how you had the next room to hers at uni, and that you and she were good friends. Then you said something about your summer break and that Elise went home to her parents. I think you said in Derbyshire. And then she came down to your parent's house in Cambridgeshire. You stopped at that point and I'm guessing it was because it was that summer when you were attacked?'

Alix nodded, taking another drink. 'Yes, you're right. Seeing Elise brought it all back. I had some really dark times after the attack and it was she who got me through university. She was the only one I could turn to. She was always there for me, even when I had one of my nightmares in the middle of the night. Without her, I don't know how I would have coped. I would never have got my degree. And I don't know if I'd have been in a fit state of mind to get into this job. You know that I used to hurt myself. She was the first person I told about that. She found me once in the bathroom and helped me.'

Hamlet knew Alix was talking about the self-inflicted cuts to her inner-thighs. He held her eyes, and although she was staring directly at him, her look was distant and he knew her thoughts were back to the moment. He responded, 'Look, I know how this has affected you. We can end this conversation here if it's hurting.'

She inhaled deeply. 'No. You said you think it may help our enquiry. I can get through it. Just fire away. If it gets too much, I'll tell you.'

'If you're sure?'

'I'm sure. Just ask me what you need to.'

'You said Elise came down to the vicarage?'

'Yes,' Alix nodded. 'We arranged for her to come and visit. She said she always wanted to visit Cambridge. I said she could stay with us for a few days. I knew my parents wouldn't mind. The vicarage had four bedrooms. So that was it sorted.

'We broke up for the holidays in late May and she came down at the end of June. She drove down. It was only supposed to be for a few days but she ended up staying over two weeks. She stayed around for three days after the attack. She went to the hospital and stopped with me while I was being examined, and came with me to the police station when I gave my statement.'

Hamlet offered a consoling look. 'I can see now why you reacted the way you did when we found her.'

'I couldn't have wished for a better friend, especially as you know how distant I became with my mum and dad after it happened. Elise did so much for me and gave me so much support.'

'Was Elise there when it happened?'

'You mean at the vicarage when I was attacked?'

Hamlet nodded.

'It was Elise who disturbed him. She came back and he escaped out of the bathroom window.' Alix broke off and looked about her as if in a daze, then she returned her gaze. 'I'd forgot about that bit. Mum and Dad had got to going to a quiz night at a pub in the next village on a regular basis and I started going with them when I visited. Well, when Elise came down, she joined us.

'We were unstoppable as a team. We won nearly every time. The second night in there she copped off with one of the local farmers sons. He was gorgeous looking, or so I can remember thinking. Dark hair, tanned, body to die for. Everything a nineteen-year-old looks for.' She let out a laugh. 'Jules, his name was. Me and Elise went to the pub most nights after they'd got together, and we'd meet up with him and his mates.

'I had a bit of a snog with one of his mates one drunken night in the car park while Elise and Jules had more than that behind one of the outbuildings. It was a great couple of weeks. Until that night.' Her voice trailed off and she lifted her eyes skyward for a few seconds before returning them. 'The night of my attack was a quiz night. That's why there was no one in the vicarage. We all went to the pub.

'Jules turned up late at the pub in his dad's Land Rover. We had just finished the quiz. We ordered another round of drinks but Elise copped out. She said Jules was going to take her for a spin.

'So off she went. We finished our drinks and then mum drove us home. We pulled up on the drive and I was busting for the loo and ran straight up to the bathroom.

'Unknown to us, the man had broken in through my dad's ground floor study. The house wasn't alarmed. It was such a quiet village. Nothing ever happened there.' She caught herself and added, 'Until that night.' She took another drink of her wine, studied the glass in front of her face for a couple of seconds and then connected her gaze back to Hamlet. 'Mum shouted up that she was going to make a drink and I shouted back down that I'd have one. I wanted to wait up for Elise coming back.

'I was just coming downstairs when I heard Mum scream and I rushed down and he was there. In the lounge. He was dressed in black and had on a ski mask. He was holding a knife, shaking it around, threatening. Mum was sitting on the settee and Dad in his chair. At first he didn't see me.' Suddenly she stopped, gasped and put a hand to her mouth.

'What's the matter, Alix?'

'I've blanked most of this out for years but it's all coming back to me now. And a lot clearer. When the police came and asked me what had happened and I went through it all, I told them that the first thing he said was "Where is it? Where's your money?" Because at the time that's what I could remember. But the first thing he actually said was, "Where is she?"

'The burglar still hadn't seen I was there at that stage. I was in the hall standing by the door. My dad gave me this look to get out of there, and that's when the man turned and saw me. I tried to run, but he was so quick. He got me by the hair and dragged me back. He started shouting at me and saying, "Is she upstairs?" At the time it didn't make sense, but you've just made me get it.' Alix stiffened. 'It was Elise, wasn't it? That's who he was after?'

'That's what's been niggling away at me ever since you mentioned her coming down to your parent's home where you were attacked. I've been wanting to ask you this, ever since you told us about Elise being hassled by one of the male students, and that she'd reported him and he'd then gone off sick. When you told us that, the first thing that sprang to mind was that it was him who'd killed her. And when you said she'd come down to stay with you, and it was then when you were attacked, it came into my thoughts that maybe it could be the same man who'd been hassling Elise and he'd got the wrong person.

'Now you've just told me this story I'm convinced he got the wrong person. He was there for Elise. I'd bet a wager on it. You know what I've been saying about the person we're looking for and his characteristic traits? Well, he fits all of them. I bet he followed her to your parent's place. He probably laid low for a while, watching the vicarage, building himself up, waiting for the right moment.

'Now I've seen Elise, there are similarities between the pair of you. Same age, roughly the same height and build, and both of you have dark hair. He could have easily got you mixed up from a distance. It's my guess he followed you all to the pub and then while you were all in there he returned to the vicarage, broke in and then waited for you all to come back, not knowing Elise had gone off with Jules.

'Alix, I think you just happened to be very unfortunate. It was never about you.'

'Jesus, Hamlet.'

Hamlet saw her hands start to shake. He reached across and grabbed hold of them. 'It's imperative we find out who it was who was hassling Elise at university. I'm sure he's the man we're after.'

SIXTEEN

It was after nine when Alix got home. Katie and Nate had dropped her off because she had ended up drinking another two glasses of wine after Hamlet had left. She had intended going straight home herself as she'd watched him leave, but the need to dull her thoughts had been more pressing and the offer by Katie to "have another" had been too hard to resist.

Now, her head was spinning. And not just with alcohol. She had spent years coping with her dark memories. A lot of that time, she had been distracted, focussing on her career, and that had been extremely helpful, although a few times there had been *that job* that had come along that had jerked her back to her past.

This was another one of those times when *that job* had pushed her over the edge again and she needed to deal with it. Locking the front door, securing it with the deadbolt and re-setting the alarm to perimeter, she decided she needed another drink. *Just one more. That's it.* To blur the images washing around inside her head and to relax her before bed.

She went about her room-to-room checks, seeing all was safe, poured herself a glass of wine from the fridge, took a sip and headed upstairs to get a shower. Before getting undressed she peered out of her bedroom window into the dark, scanning the street outside, concentrating her searching eyes in all the dark recesses. All was quiet.

She closed the curtains and pulled off her clothes, slipped on her dressing gown, took another sip of wine and headed to the bathroom. Turning on the shower, she wiped off her foundation, finished her wine, brushed her teeth and climbed into the shower.

As the jets of water hit the back of her neck and shoulders, she cranked up the temperature to what was just bearable and stayed under the hot water for five minutes as it cleansed her body, reddening her skin. She could feel the water trickling over the scars on her thighs, nudging her thoughts back to that night.

All that time she had been thinking that what had happened to her had been something to do with what she might have done. Now she knew it wasn't, thanks to Hamlet. She had never been the intended target. It had been Elise who had brought him to her parent's home. Elise! And now she was dead. She would never be able to talk to her about it.

Tears sprang from her eyes and ran down her cheeks, joining the rivulets of hot water that battered her fatigued body. She felt utterly drained, yet she knew she would have difficulty getting off to sleep tonight. She needed her mirtazapine. It had been a long time since she'd taken any but tonight was one of those nights when she needed a couple.

Towelling herself dry, she slipped her dressing gown back on, wrapped it tightly around her, and made her way back downstairs, where she rinsed out her wine glass, replenished it with water and took two mirtazapine.

Downing the last of the water she went to the sink and washed her glass, catching her faint reflection in the window that overlooked her back garden. For a moment she tried to study her image staring back. She was at a low ebb tonight and she wondered if it showed in her face.

At that moment, she caught a movement beyond her reflection in the garden. She immediately stepped back and turned off the light, taking deep breaths. Her heart was racing.

In the dark, she edged back to the kitchen window and peered into her garden. She could pick out the lawn and the rear wall and she scoured right and left. Nothing. No movement.

She cursed herself. Her paranoia was running away with her again. It had happened before. Many times. The conversation with Hamlet had once more raised the demons.

As she stepped back, the ringing of her phone made her jump. Her chest tightened. She picked up her phone. It was an unknown caller. She let it ring off and was about to put it down when it rang again. Unknown.

She was about to answer it when a loud knock came from her front door, once more making her jump. Her caller? She inched her way towards the hallway, training her ears on the front door.

Another knock. This time louder. She stopped in the hall doorway. 'Who is it?' she called.

SEVENTEEN

Hamlet was just entering the clearing in front of his cabin after returning from his early morning walk when his phone rang. He expected it to be Alix but the number on the screen wasn't one he recognised. With slight apprehension, he answered. He was surprised to hear Katie's voice. She sounded anxious.

'Have you spoken with Alix this morning?' she asked.

'No, I haven't. Why?'

'I arranged to pick her up for work because she left her car at the pub last night after Nate and I dropped her off. She isn't answering her door and I can hear her phone inside her house when I've rung it. Did she seem all right when she was talking with you last night?'

'She was fine.'

'Listen, Hamlet, can you join me? I'm a bit worried about her. She'd had a bit to drink when we dropped her off but I've seen her in worse states and she doesn't usually miss work with a hangover. I'm wondering if she might have fallen or something. I'm going to keep ringing her and see if I can rouse her. Can you come?'

'I'll be there as soon as I can.'

When Hamlet pulled up outside Alix's house, Katie was by the front door looking agitated. As soon as he opened the car door, she headed for him.

'This is not like her at all. She's still not answering her phone and I can hear it ringing downstairs. I've spoken with one of the neighbours, and she's not seen her this morning, and the curtains are still closed. I've rung work, just in case she got a lift in from someone else, but she's not there. I've checked through the letterbox and she's not fallen down the stairs.'

'What do you want to do? Break in?'

'I don't know what other options there are. I've been banging on the door, and she's not responded. And I've never known Alix go anywhere without her phone.'

Hamlet dipped his head toward the front door. 'It'd be no use trying to get in through that. It's got at least two locks and it's fitted with deadbolts from what I remember. It'd be like trying to break into Fort Knox.'

'That's why I'm a bit worried. I know how safety conscious Alix is, but when I tried it this morning there was quite a bit of movement. I think she's just left it on the latch.'

Unease suddenly gripped Hamlet. He knew Alix always went through a safety routine at home and that included double-locking and deadbolting both the front and back doors whenever she was in. He hurried down the short path and tested the front door with his shoulder. It immediately shifted in its frame. Katie was right.

He said, 'I think this will give. We'll worry about what it'll cost to fix later.'

Tight-lipped, Katie gave a nod of approval.

Taking a step back, Hamlet launched himself at the door. It shot open first time, sending him crashing into the hall, his outspread hands only just stopping him from hitting the carpet face-first. A sharp pain jolted up from his wrists, making him wince.

'You okay, Hamlet?' Katie said rushing in behind him.

He rolled onto his side, letting out a groan. 'I wasn't expecting that.'

153

'I can see,' she returned, letting out a laugh. 'You'd be no good on a raid. We'd be climbing all over you now to get to the suspect.'

He pushed himself onto his knees, rubbing his hands.

'You take downstairs and I'll do up. See if she's here,' Katie said, striding over him and jogging up the stairs.

Hamlet picked himself up and headed into the lounge. It was in gloom, the curtains closed, but he could still pick out the shapes of his surroundings and he could see Alix wasn't in here.

He headed into the back. In the kitchen-cum-diner sunlight streamed in and everything seemed to be as he last remembered. There was nothing out of place and no sign that Alix had come to any harm. His eyes came to a halt when he spotted her phone lying next to her bag on the worktop. Beside her bag was an open book and slotted between the middle fold was a pink wedding invitation.

Suddenly the hairs at the back of his neck bristled, and in that same moment Katie shouted down, 'She's not here, Hamlet.'

Not shifting his eyes, he called back, 'You need to come down and look at this.'

Within half an hour cops were crawling all over Alix's normally quiet street. It had been sealed off at either end and neighbour's doors were being banged on and gardens and alleyways searched. The helicopter was up making a terrible racket, hovering around and people were out on their doorsteps gawking.

Hamlet stood at the end of the path looking up and down the road storing snapshots of activity to memory. It wouldn't be long before the press arrived. More publicity at a time when they didn't need it. Especially with 'The Wedding Killer's' latest victim being a detective, working on the case.

Hamlet was worried. His and Alix's conversation yesterday evening had been about the killer. Now he wondered if he may have got it wrong. Had Alix been the intended victim all along? Has he been stalking Alix because of her involvement in the hunt for him following his abduction of Hayley Stevenson?

Hamlet had rewound yesterday's scene when they had been sat outside the pub, trying to recall if there was anyone sat on their own on one of the nearby benches. His recollection was that they were all small groups, mainly workers who had stopped by for a few drinks before heading home.

'Katie tells me she thinks Alix has been taken by our man?'

Lauren's voice made him jump. He turned to face her marching towards him. In her arms she was carrying sealed bags of forensic suits. She slung him one. 'Put this on, Hamlet,' she said. 'I know you've already been inside but Alix's home is a crime-scene now. I want you to lead me through everything. I've bumped into Katie at the end of the road and she's given me the gist of things, including you finding the same wedding invitation that our other victims have received. I've asked her to wait for CSI to get here, so you're in the hot seat while we do this.'

Hamlet climbed into his all-in-one, and fitting the mask in place and pulling up the hood he made his way along the path to the front door. 'Well, I got here around 7.30, boss. Katie was here when I arrived.'

'Yes, she's told me that she dropped Alix off last night and had arranged to pick her up this morning, so she could collect her car before work. Apparently, she had a bit to drink yesterday evening and so cadged a lift with Katie.'

155

Hamlet nodded. 'That's what Katie told me.' He stopped at the front door. It was open. Exactly as he and Katie had left it after breaking in. The metal hasp for the Yale lock was lying in the middle of the hallway.

Lauren drew up beside Hamlet and pointed to the hasp. 'Katie told me you had to break in?'

'Yes,' Hamlet nodded. 'That's down to me.'

'Katie said the door was only on the Yale when you got here. Apparently, Alix normally sets two locks and a deadlock bolt on when she's in the house?'

'Yes, that's what I've observed when I've been here. And she normally sets the alarm to perimeter when she's in. That wasn't on either when I broke open the door.'

'A bit overly security conscious?'

Hamlet saw the quizzical look on Lauren's face. Alix's attack had left her fearful of having an intruder in her home, so she had installed extra security measures. He wasn't prepared to divulge what she had shared with him in confidence, so he answered, 'I've been extra vigilant since James Harry Benson tried to kill me. Alix is probably the same.'

Lauren delivered a sharp nod. 'Yes, I guess so.' She remained on the doorstep, gazing up and down the hall. 'Does that tell you anything then, Hamlet?'

'I have given it some thought, boss. It's certainly not like Alix to lock the door on just the Yale. That's completely out of character, and I'm thinking whoever took Alix probably did that on his way out. That's why the alarm wasn't set.

'But what I haven't fathomed out is how he got into the house without forcing his way in. As you've noticed, Alix is extremely security conscious. She always double-locks the house, Yale and mortice, and she always sets the alarm without fail. It's a force of habit. The same goes for the back door.

That's got a mortice lock and two deadbolts fitted. That's still secure.

'Katie told me that she didn't actually see Alix go into the house last night. She and Nate dropped her off at the front of the house and then drove off before she went in, so even if her attacker was lying in wait, he can't have attacked her before she got in because of the situation with the front door and the alarm. The fact that only her Yale was on this morning means she's unlocked the front door and deactivated the alarm.

'I had thought maybe he took her by surprise before she's been able to lock up and reset the alarm, but then her handbag and phone are in the kitchen. She'll have had to make her way through the house. The only thing I can think at the moment is that she answered the door to someone she knew, or someone that she didn't consider a threat, and then been taken by surprise.

'Certainly, no alarm sounded last night. Katie and I have spoken with the immediate neighbours. And there's no sign of forced entry to the house or of a struggle. Mind you, we know from speaking with Hayley that he used a taser on her to subdue her. There's a strong possibility he did the same to Alix the moment she opened the door.'

'Any thoughts on who this person is Hamlet?'

'Not at the moment, boss. I'm still trying to process it all.'

'And what about this wedding invitation?' Lauren asked, setting off along the hall to the kitchen.

'I found that next to her bag and phone. It's in a book, which was left open. And this is the interesting thing. It's a crime fiction book, and it's been left open at a page where the female victim is being abducted.'

EIGHTEEN

The focus of the evening briefing was on Alix's abduction. The entire force was involved in some way in looking for her. Task Force and the dog section were at the heart of it, some of the resources returning to Bradfield to carry out a search of the surrounding moorland in case The Wedding Killer — as he was now known — had retreated to familiar ground.

Forensic work was still going on at Alix's Victorian semi. The hallway and kitchen had been photographed and videoed, as had upstairs, and the images had been collated and plastered over a fresh whiteboard together with a photograph of Alix.

As Hamlet danced his eyes along the pictures, he suddenly realised Alix's bed had not been slept in, suggesting she had been abducted not long after getting in. A shot of the kitchen sink showed a single glass upside down on the drainer. So that suggested that she hadn't entertained anyone, but it seemed as if she had opened the door to someone she trusted.

Apart from her neighbours, her parents and the people she worked with, he couldn't think who else that person could be. He dismissed both of Alix's immediate neighbours. They were in their sixties and both widows. If it hadn't been for the wedding invitation placed in a page where the narrative described the brutal abduction of a young woman, they wouldn't have had a clue what had happened to her. Or who had taken her.

The Wedding Killer clearly wanted them to know it was him. Discovering who that person was and finding him — and Alix — was now the immediate priority.

On that front, the MIT team were exhausted. Every spare detective had been working on house-to-house inquiries in Alix's neighbourhood, persuading residents to let them search their homes and outbuildings as well as enquiring what they had seen or heard the previous night.

So far, it had reaped one lead. A householder four doors away had found a five-second snippet on his house CCTV of Alix being limply supported in a bear-hug by a slim man in dark clothing and dark woolly hat past his home at 21.57 p.m. This was roughly half an hour after Katie had dropped her off.

Whilst everyone could see the woman was Alix, there was no way they could identify who her captor was. The camera it had been captured on was fastened high up on the side of the house, facing downward, and the man's hat completely shielded his face. It was even difficult to judge his height, not only because of the camera's position but also because he was struggling with heaving Alix's sagging body along and so was bent at the shoulders. He did appear to be strong though for his build.

Sadly, they had found no other cameras nearby, and so there were no more sightings, though everyone was of the opinion that she had more than likely been transported away in the culprit's vehicle, and so they were now working through footage from ANPR traffic cameras around Alix's location obtaining details of vehicles during the timeframe.

Lauren recapped events, calling on Katie Turner to detail the car journey from the pub to Alix's home. Nate Fox had also been in the car and he corroborated Katie's recollection. Both said that Alix had been very quiet on the way home and they had put it down to the sad event of finding the body of her friend in the bunker, as well as having drunk far more than she normally did.

Hamlet listened intently. Whilst he knew that was all true, he also knew more to the story, which he was keeping to himself for now. Katie also led on what she and Hamlet had discovered that morning at Alix's house, whereupon Lauren took back the reins to summarise the present stage of enquiries.

Upon finishing, she said, 'One of the things Alix revealed after the discovery of Hayley and the bodies is that her friend Elise had been harassed by a male student on the same journalist course at university and had reported him. I tasked that out for enquiries into finding who that person was. Has it been done?'

Detective Nick Lewis pushed up his hand. 'That's me, boss. The university finally got back to me this afternoon with the information. I spoke with the admin supervisor and she tells me that they only have a summarised account of Elise's complaint held on the computer system. The original paperwork looks as though it's been disposed of — that they only keep complaints of this nature for seven years, then its shredded.

'The allegation she made was that a student called Matthew Denton was stalking her via social media, and she was also receiving emails from him to the effect that he fancied her and would like to go out with her.

'When these became abusive, she made a complaint to the principal, Professor Williams, and the note on the system is that Matthew Denton denied everything.

'However, Professor Williams was concerned about Matthew's behaviour and he was referred for counselling and suspended pending an investigation into Elise's complaint.

'There is nothing on the system as to whether he went for counselling but we do know he did not return to complete his degree. I have called the university back to see if I can speak with Professor Williams, but I've been told he's retired. I've asked if they can contact him so I can speak with him. I'm still waiting for the call back.'

As Nick finished his report Nate interjected with, 'Boss, I don't know if it's the same person but I knew a Matthew Denton when I was at uni studying law. He had a room in the shared house me and two other students rented. I never got to know him that well because he was on a different course. He came for a drink with us a couple of times when we went into town, but he was sort of an oddball character, from what I remember. A bit deep. He kept himself very much to himself, and to be honest we avoided him if we could.'

'Well, Alix did tell us that Elise mentioned he was suffering from depression. It could be the same person. The name's not a common one. Can you chase that up, Nate?'

Hamlet stuck up his hand. 'If it's any help, boss, I can do the follow-up checks to see if he went for counselling. I know who to contact for case reports.'

'Thank you, Hamlet. That will be useful,' Lauren responded. 'And thank you everyone for your input.' Clasping her hands together, she added, 'Alix has been missing for less than 24 hours and we all know the first 48 hours are crucial. We must stay focussed and positive. We found Hayley and we now have a strong lead with this Matthew Denton character. Let's see if we can trace him pronto and pull out all the stops to get Alix back.'

NINETEEN

'Matthew Denton has disappeared off the face of the earth, boss,' said Nate at morning briefing the following day. 'His full name is Matthew Charles Denton. He was born in 1990, to parents Hayden and Jo, and lived in Hope, Derbyshire, until their deaths in a climbing accident in Wales in 2007, when he went to live with his grandmother in Shiregreen. She died of cancer in 2011, and from there we seem to have lost him.

'The story that Elise told Alix about his life seems to be true. He went to Sheffield University in 2008, enrolling for a BA in Journalism Studies, and his student file has a record of the complaints made by Elise. There are two — the first one was in January of 2009, and the second in May the same year, when he was suspended. After his grandmother died, he has gone off grid. I can't find a record of him anywhere after that. I have checked Works and Pensions, HMRC and benefits. Nothing.'

'Could he have changed his name?' Lauren enquired.

'That's what I'm thinking. I've sent an email to the National Archives to check.'

'And you said he shared a house with you and your friends when you were at uni, Nate?'

'Yes. He was the first to answer an ad we put on the noticeboard in the student's bar. He rented the loft space. We didn't see that much of him to be honest. As I said before, I was studying law and he was doing journalism, and our lectures were at different times.

'Also, we were a year in front of him. And he didn't always stay at the house, and that makes sense now with his gran being ill. He was more than likely looking after her, flitting between her home and our place. We did invite him out into town a couple of times, and he came out for a beer with us, but as I say, he was a bit on the quiet side. He didn't act strange or anything, and I never heard about the complaints against him.'

'Do you have any photos of him from back then?' asked Lauren.

Nate shook his head. 'No, sorry, boss. Like I say, he wasn't part of my crowd. We only asked him out because we felt sorry for him. We had no idea about what he had been up to with Elise.'

'Never mind. It was a long shot. Okay, you keep digging away. It's really important we find him pronto. We're now into the second day since Alix was taken. We need to find where she is.' She ran her eyes over her team. Many heads were nodding. She switched her gaze to Hamlet. 'Hamlet, you had the task of finding out if Matthew Denton went for counselling. Have you got anything?'

Hamlet shifted in his seat. 'I have, boss. I went through the normal channels to start with and made requests for his casefile but I also asked who was involved in his assessment and I've found out there were two people. One of those was Dr Ian Whitton, who you'll recall was my colleague at Moor Lodge.'

Hamlet paused as a phantom memory floated to the surface. The last thing he wanted to do was revisit the chain of events caused by Dr Whitton, when James Harry Benson, who had been previously been under Dr Whitton's care, had escaped.

Blinking away the intrusive thoughts and taking a deep breath, he continued, 'What is interesting is that Dr Whitton wasn't the first choice psychiatrist recommended for Matthew Denton. He was assigned to him following a series of disturbing episodes with Denton's first psychiatrist, a Dr Isobel Casey.

'Dr Casey had six sessions with Matthew, the first of which were about his childhood, the death of his parents and how that affected him and life with his grandmother, who had cancer. After that Dr Casey focussed on the complaints made by Elise.

'The case notes make mention that Matthew admitted having affections for Elise but he vehemently denied stalking her, blaming someone else, who he says, "wanted to get him into trouble but he didn't know why."

'The really interesting bit is that Dr Casey also received cards, silent phone calls and flowers placed under her windscreen wipers, which she believed all came from Matthew within weeks of seeing him. There is also mention of Matthew following her to a bar where she was meeting her boyfriend for a drink. She became so concerned that she halted the sessions and applied for a job up in Newcastle, where she originated from, just to get away from him. She now works at the Royal Victoria Infirmary in Newcastle.'

'Can I just halt you there, Hamlet?' Lauren interrupted. 'Was Matthew questioned about his behaviour towards Dr Casey?'

'Yes. She challenged him about following her to the pub and his response was that it was a coincidence. He had gone there to meet up with friends. He was asked about sending the cards and making the phone calls in his last session with Dr Whitton in 2009.

'He denied everything. And after that session he never returned to university. The final part of Matthew Denton's case notes is the diagnosis. He was diagnosed with de Clérambault's Syndrome, a rare delusional disorder named after the French psychiatrist Gaëtan Gatian de Clérambault. I have heard of this syndrome but never personally met anyone diagnosed with it. It's also known as Erotomania.

'The condition is characterised by an individual's belief that another person is intensely in love with them. They will often do anything to grab their target's attention — send gifts, cards, make phone calls and even stalk. Does this sound familiar? It applies to every one of our victims. And that leads me to believe he has a narcissistic personality disorder as well. This is a complex condition often characterized by an inflated sense of self-importance, lack of empathy, and a deep need for constant attention or admiration.'

'So, could this make him dangerous?' Lauren said.

Hamlet met his DI's serious look. 'Yes, boss.'

'That makes it even more urgent we pull out all the stops to find Alix.' Lauren clapped her hands and grasped them together. 'Hamlet, thank you for this information. It's been very helpful. Very helpful indeed. To follow up I want you to go up to Newcastle and have an in-depth chat with Dr Casey about her sessions with Matthew. See if she can offer anything else that may help us trace him.

'The rest of the team, see if we can find addresses for Matthew Denton. I'm particularly interested in where his grandmother lived. We need to track him down urgently.'

TWENTY

Alix came to with a start, letting out a groan as a sharp pain rippled through her left arm. She was lying on it and tried to move, letting out another moan as the cramp in her upper arm smarted, sending a throbbing sensation straight down to her wrist.

Her arms were fastened tightly at the wrists behind her back but she couldn't see how. She could feel that her hands had lost some of their sensation and she started to ease them apart. Instantly, an electric current shot to her fingertips, making her flinch and grimace. She tried to move her legs, but they were also trussed securely and she slowly eased herself over to get a better look at what was holding them.

The movement caused her pain. She was so stiff. As she slowly raised her head, visions of her capture came back. He'd tasered her the moment she'd opened the door. Taken her completely by surprise. All she could remember about him was the dark clothing and ski mask he was wearing. But why the disguise? She knew him. He'd called her name. She recognised his voice.

Why me? She let out an angry shout and thrashed out with her legs, kicking the air. Her knee joints clicked, and a fresh pain made her gasp.

Where the fuck am I? It certainly wasn't the bunker. There had been no light in there. Here, there was slivers of it, poking between thin slits of whatever was sealing her tomb.

As her eyesight adjusted, she could make out that she was laying in some kind of concrete trench. It smelled of grease and oil and reminded her of an old garage pit. She rolled over a little more to get a better look at her what was holding her legs. Circulation was returning to her body. The discomfort was easing. Within a few seconds she was able to raise them, getting them to almost 90 degrees, and in the limited light she saw her ankles were secured with black cable ties. Two at least. She guessed the same was fastening her wrists.

As she rested back on her legs, shuffling her bottom to a more comfortable position, she wondered if he was up there, listening to her struggles. Having a laugh at her expense. She could feel the anger building up inside her and she lashed out with her legs, smashing her feet against the concrete wall.

A stinging pain shot straight up her legs making her yelp. 'You bastard!' she snapped. 'You're going down for this. Mark my fucking words.'

Cramps in her arms bucked Alix out of sleep. She must have drifted off. She blinked open her eyes, cringing at the shooting pains travelling from her elbows to her wrists.

Moving slowly, she rolled onto her side and pulled back her arms. Just trying to straighten them was painful. Her throat and mouth were dry. So were her lips, and her tongue felt swollen.

He'd left Hayley with water. Drugged water. She'd welcome that right now, her mouth and throat hurt so much. But he'd left nothing. *Bastard!* How long could someone live without water?

She pushed herself back against the pit wall, pressing herself against the concrete, manoeuvring her bottom so she could slip her legs beneath to give her more purchase to try and raise herself. More pain, this time through her legs, made her twitch and fall sideways, headbutting the floor.

The sting that shot through her skull sent stars cascading behind her eyes, making her cry out. For the best part of a minute she lay there, trying to bring back her vision that was swirling around, making her feel sick.

Alix started to sob, but the sound stuck in her dry throat, making her wretch. Was this how she was going to die? Thirsty and in such pain?

Up above, the sudden sound of a noisy diesel engine made her spring open her eyes. It sounded like a lorry, or a wagon of some type. It wasn't too far away and coming closer according to the increasing noise of the engine.

She held her breath, concentrated her hearing, and caught the hissing sound of compressed air as it braked. It was stopping and not too far away. Her heart started racing. Who was this?

A door banged, quickly followed by another. Two people? They were out of the vehicle. She started to yell but the sound came out as a cough. Her throat was swollen and so sore. She wanted to scream but couldn't. *Please help me.*

Hamlet was changing out of his jeans and T-shirt and into his suit following his woodland walk when his mobile rang. It was Lauren. The clock in his bedroom told him it was 6.32 a.m. *Something's happened,* he told himself as he answered, 'Morning, boss.'

'Morning, Hamlet. Are you on your way in?'

'Just getting changed into my work clothes. Has something happened?'

'You could say that. We've found Alix.'

'She's been found!'

'In a disused garage at Attercliffe. Two men dismantling machinery at some engineering works next to it found her. She was tied up in one of the pits. She's severely dehydrated like Hayley was but she's responding well according to the hospital.

A couple of uniform are babysitting her, and I've spoken with her briefly an hour ago. She's named Matthew Denton as her attacker. She told me he came to her house the other night and tasered her when she answered the door. She's itching to get into work to have five minutes with him. Typical Alix.'

'That's great news, boss. I'll be there in half an hour, or should I go to the hospital first?'

'No, I want you in here. You'd just be hanging around twiddling your thumbs at the hospital. I want you to conduct your first interview with Denton. Katie will be leading but I want your observation and input especially given your knowledge about his condition.'

'You've got Matthew Denton?'

'Locked up this morning. We did a dawn raid. He still lives at the house that belonged to his gran. He inherited it. He's changed his name, like we thought, but he registered it through his council tax. We found where he lived late last night and did the raid this morning. Forensics have just started searching it.'

'What's he changed his name to?'

'You won't believe this, but he's been under our noses all along. It's none other than Matt Ross, the crime correspondent for the *Sheffield Telegraph*. Remember him?'

'The one asking all the awkward questions at the press briefings?'

'One and the same. And we know why now, don't we? When you get here, we'll have a quick scrum-down, and then you and Katie can get off and interview him.'

Hamlet and Katie left a buzzing MIT office shortly after 10 a.m. to travel to the custody suite where Matthew Denton was being held.

Katie had an interview strategy drafted and Hamlet had probing questions relating to Matthew's condition firmly fixed in his head. They were both ready to duel with The Wedding Killer.

It was a good hour before they got into the interview room. Matthew had engaged in a lengthy meeting with his lawyer, and when they walked into the warm and stuffy room, the defence lawyer was seated next to him, pen hovering over a yellow legal pad.

Matthew was wearing a grey sweater and joggers, standard prison issue. His tanned complexion and curly straw-coloured hair, touching his collar, gave him an almost surfer-boy look, and his clean-shaven face displayed an innocent little-boy-lost look that made him appear younger than his thirty years. Nothing like a serial killer.

Matthew and his lawyer looked up, their eyes following the detectives as they took the two seats opposite, switching their gazes to the pile of papers and three evidence bags that Katie carefully laid facedown on the desk between them. Matthew centred his focus on Hamlet, watching him take off his jacket and place it around his chair, and as Hamlet made himself comfortable, he said, 'Aren't you Dr… Mottrell?'

Hamlet knew that the journalist had been about to call to him by the nickname he had been given by the local media whilst still a suspect in his family's murders — Doctor Death — and had just caught himself. 'Correct, Matthew,' he replied.

'But what're you doing here?'

'You'll be surprised to learn I recovered from my pillorying by the press, who wrongly accused me of murder, and I've decided to pursue justice for my family by becoming a detective.' Hamlet delivered the sentence with a smile.

Matthew returned a smile of his own. 'Well, this is a turn up for the books. I might just do a story about you, Dr Mottrell. Our readers would love to hear your side of things.'

'Not anytime soon I don't think.'

'Matthew,' Katie interrupted, 'I don't think you seem to grasp the seriousness of the situation.'

Matthew shot his gaze her way, his face taking on a serious look. 'Oh, I do, detective. Believe me I do. As Dr Mottrell has just alluded to, being an innocent man, wrongly accused of doing something you haven't done, is a very serious position to find oneself in. This morning I was dragged out of my bed by your stormtroopers and told I was being arrested for abducting one of your detectives, and I am severely pissed off over it. When you finally realise you have got this drastically wrong our readers are going to find out exactly what policing has boiled down to in South Yorkshire.'

'And I'm sure nothing I will say will persuade you against that. In the meantime, Matthew, you'll be pleased to hear that I will be conducting an interview with you, during which I will present a series of questions to you, together with evidence of guilt that resulted in you being "dragged out of your bed by stormtroopers," as you have so dramatically put it.'

Hamlet noted that Katie accentuated the word 'guilt' as she delivered her retort and found it quite amusing. He himself had been subjected to interrogation by her when he had been a suspect, and whilst he hadn't been too impressed at being at the mercy of her vicious questions, he was now in a completely different position, and had to admit he was suitably impressed with her style of interview. He could see that no matter how much Matthew was going to attempt to rattle her, he wouldn't succeed. He made himself comfortable.

'Your lawyer has already advised you of how this interview will be conducted, Matthew?' Katie continued.

Matthew glanced sideways at his lawyer, a woman in her early forties with shoulder-length dark hair, expensively dressed in a blue fitted jacket and trousers with white blouse. She came from a well-known city practice who specialised in defending clients with money and with a reputation for suing the police over malpractice. He was well represented. He returned his gaze to Katie and nodded. 'I have been advised, yes.'

'And I'm sure she will have advised you to "make no comment," and that is your own prerogative, however, if you have nothing to hide it comes across better to a jury if you give reasonable answers to reasonable questions. I'm sure you will have experience of this as a journalist covering trials, won't you?' Katie's face was deadpan.

'I have been advised by my lawyer and I can assure you I will vehemently deny these ludicrous allegations. I've never attacked anyone in my life, never mind abduct a detective. Why would I do that?'

'Well, we'll see, Matthew. Shan't we?' Katie lined up her paperwork, leaving her evidence bags face down. She glanced at the notes she had prepared and then put Matthew in her sights. 'What do you know of Detective Alix Rainbow?'

He shrugged. 'I don't know her. I know the name because of her involvement with Dr Mottrell here. She investigated his family's murders. I was deputising for Kieran Crofts, the crime correspondent for our sister paper, when he was found murdered in Dr Mottrell's cabin. I took over his work and her name was mentioned in his file.'

'So, you're saying you don't know her personally then?'
'No.'
'What about where she lives?'

'I have no idea.'

'Two nights ago, did you call her on her phone and speak with her?'

Matthew's eyebrows knitted together. 'No. I've never spoken to her. I've just told you I don't know her.'

'And you didn't go to her home two nights ago?'

'No. I've no idea where she lives. And why would I go to her home, even if I did?'

'Where were you two nights ago between the hours of nine p.m. and midnight?'

'At home, watching the telly. I always watch the ten o'clock news and then go to bed and read for a while. You could say I lead a pretty boring life, but it suits me. I got used to that type of life looking after my gran when she was ill with lung cancer.'

'You watched the news and read you say?'

'Yes. It's my routine.'

'What kind of books do you read?'

'I read crime. Mainly fiction.'

'You've just mentioned your gran, and that you looked after her when she had cancer, do you mind if we digress for a moment and talk about her?'

The lawyer asked, 'Is this relevant, detective?'

Katie kept her face neutral. 'It could be. It does relate to some information we received about Matthew from a few years back that's in connection with an ongoing investigation of ours.' Before the lawyer could raise any objections Katie spun her gaze back to Matthew. 'If any of my questions get uncomfortable, Matthew, just say, but I would appreciate if you can help me out.'

Matthew gave her a puzzled look. 'Sure.'

'When did your gran get ill?'

'I went to live with her in 2007. My parents died in a climbing accident in Llanberis Pass when I was seventeen, so she took me in. I was close to my gran. She was my mum's mum. My other gran lives in France with my grandad. I've only seen them a couple of times when we went on holiday there.

'My Granny Ross was the one I regularly saw. I used to visit her quite a lot when I was younger. Stayed with her a few times when my mum and dad worked away. My dad worked for an oil company and did a lot of work overseas. His work could take him away for up to six months and my mum used to go with him. That's when I stayed with her.

'She always struggled with her health. She suffered from COPD because of smoking. Her breathing got worse when I went to live with her and that's when she was diagnosed with lung cancer. I took her for all her treatment and looked after her until she went into the hospice. She died within a week of going in.'

'I'm sorry to hear that, Matthew. That can't have been easy for you as a teenager.'

'It wasn't.'

'And you were studying at Sheffield University at the time that happened, I believe?'

'Yes. Journalism Studies.'

'Yes, that's what we've been told. Do you mind me asking something about when you were at university?'

'Sure.'

Hamlet was listening intently. He was fascinated by the way Katie's questioning technique was slowly luring Matthew in. He was learning a lot.

Katie said, 'We've been told that another student complained about your behaviour when you were at university. That you stalked her on social media and sent her emails that weren't appropriate.'

Matthew's face went beetroot. 'Just what is this? First, you're talking to me about abducting a detective. This Alix Rainbow woman. And now you're questioning me about what happened with Elise ten years ago. Which I already told the psychiatrist I was sent to for counselling was nothing to do with me. I was set up.'

'You've just said the name Elise?'

'Yes, Elise Lewis. She was on my journalism course. We were friends until she received all that rubbish supposedly from me. Then she just changed. I was accused of bombarding her with emails, saying that I fancied her. But it wasn't me. I told my counsellor all that. I was treated unfairly by the university. They just wouldn't listen to anything I said in my defence. Instead, they suspended me, and in the end I left. I had to. No one would believe me. I went to Lincoln University to finish my studies.'

'Did you speak to Elise about this?'

'Initially I did. I told her it wasn't me. But then she made another complaint. I was told not to talk to her. That was when they suspended me.'

'Is that when you changed your name to Matthew Ross?'

'No. That was after I decided to leave and finish my studies at another university. I took my mum's maiden name. It was the only way I could start afresh. I kept it when I came back to Sheffield for work.'

'This psychiatrist you went to see for counselling. What was their name?'

'Dr Casey,' he answered. 'I was forced to go and see her by the university. They suspended me and said they'd see how I went on. I went reluctantly but I have to say she helped me a

175

lot. She gave me some medication to help me relax and sleep at night. She also listened when I told her that I thought someone was setting me up over Elise. I thought someone had hacked into my accounts. I had to change all the passwords. I told her that.'

'But didn't Dr Casey also make a complaint about you, Matthew?'

'Apparently. The first time I became aware of it was when I received a letter from the hospital saying I wouldn't be seeing her anymore and I was to talk to them about a complaint she had made about me. I rang them, and they told me I'd been referred to Dr Whitton and that he would be continuing my counselling. I learned she'd left Sheffield and gone to work for another NHS authority.'

'Weren't you told anything about her complaint against you?'

'Not until I went to see Dr Whitton. I couldn't believe what he told me. It was similar to the allegations made by Elise, that I was stalking her. She'd said I'd sent her cards and made silent phone calls, and left flowers under her windscreen wipers. She also said I'd followed her to the pub when she'd gone there to meet her boyfriend. Now that was partly true. I had gone to the pub, and did see her there, but I'd gone there to meet up with friends. It had been arranged. I wasn't following her as she'd alleged.'

'So, what did you think about the allegations Dr Casey made against you?'

'I didn't know what to think. It was rubbish as far as I was concerned. But then I'd got to thinking that someone had it in for me. After all, this was the second occasion when things had been done in my name.'

'So, you're saying the allegations by Dr Casey and Elise Lewis had nothing to do with you?'

'Of course not. I'm not that kind of person.'

'And have you been in contact with Elise Lewis since you left Sheffield University?'

'No, sadly. I would have liked to explain things and make her believe me but I decided to draw a line under things once I'd made the decision to quit. I had an opportunity to start my life afresh and so I put all that behind me. I worked for a paper in Lincoln for a while until a reporter's job came up at the *Sheffield Telegraph* six years ago. I applied for it and got it. I'd rented my gran's house out while I'd been in Lincoln and then took it back once I'd got the job. I've been there ever since.'

'Okay, Matthew, thank you for that. We might need to come back to this, but can I go back to Detective Alix Rainbow?'

'If you insist, but I've already answered your questions about her. I don't know her and I never went to her house the other night.'

'Yes, I've noted that and thank you for your answers, but I've just got a few more questions and then we're done.' Katie looked down at her notes.

Hamlet had been keeping a keen eye on Matthew during questioning, noting his verbal responses as well as his non-verbal communication. Katie had done a good job with the interview but so far Matthew's had side-stepped any admission of guilt to any of the accusations. He'd done a good job on masking his facial emotions as well.

Raising her eyes from her notes, Katie said, 'What would you say, Matthew, if I told you that Detective Rainbow has told us that two nights ago she received calls from you on her mobile and then you knocked on her front door?'

'What? That's a lie! I've told you twice now, I don't know Detective Alix Rainbow.'

'Detective Rainbow also states that when she asked who was at her door, she heard your voice say it was you, and that you needed to talk to her. When she answered the door, she was tasered and the next day she woke up tied up in a car pit in a disused garage, where she was found last night.'

Matthew almost shot out of his seat. He banged his hands down hard on the desk, shouting, 'That's absurd! That is a complete lie!'

Katie never changed her expression. She reached forward and turned over the three exhibit bags she had brought into interview. In the first was a black taser. In the second was a bunch of black plastic cable ties, and in the third a handful of blank pink wedding invitations. Looking straight at Matthew she said, 'How do you account for these being found in your cellar this morning, then?'

TWENTY-ONE

Alix was in a private side room at the same hospital Hayley had been in. Hamlet said good evening to the constable on guard duty and entered Alix's room. He found her propped up in bed with earphones on. She greeted him with a smile and pulled out her earphones.

'I hope you've come with good news?' she said.

'I've brought grapes if that's any help?' he responded, laying the punnet beside her and pulling up a chair.

'Why am I not surprised? You are so predictable.'

Hamlet smiled as he sank into the chair, running a clinical eye over her. A cannula was still in the back of her hand, though no saline drip was attached, and he couldn't help but notice the angry red weal around each wrist where she had been cable-tied. Physically, she looked well. Her face had colour and the usual sparkle in her eyes shone brightly, though her lips gave away her ordeal of dehydration; they were heavily cracked. He knew that wouldn't last long after a couple of days of fluids. 'What does the doctor say?' he asked.

'I'm just waiting for him to come round. I asked if I could go home a couple of hours ago and the nurse says he needs to check me over and, if I'm fit, I can go.'

'Looking at you, I think that will be a yes.'

'I hope so. I'm bored. I hate hospitals. They're full of sick people.'

Hamlet chuckled.

'Anyway, enough about my welfare. I want to know how you've got on with Matthew Denton. Lauren called in this afternoon to check on me and told me you and Katie were interviewing him. She told me about him living under an assumed name. Matt Ross the reporter. Can you believe it? No wonder he knew about Hayley being a dancer. Did he cough?'

Hamlet straightened his face. 'Sorry, no, Alix. He denied everything. Katie did a great interview but he had an answer for every question.'

'The boss told me they'd found a taser, cable ties and some wedding invitations in his house. What did he say about those?'

'Says he's been stitched up. We planted the stuff.'

'You're joking?'

Hamlet shook his head. 'I'm not. We told him and his lawyer it had been found by forensics and he just said he'd never seen them before and they weren't his.'

'What about him ringing me up?'

'Says it wasn't him. He insists he doesn't know you or where you live.'

'Where is he now?'

'He's still locked up. They're bedding him down for the night and he'll be interviewed again tomorrow once they've finished going over his place. Forensics still hadn't finished when we all left. They're also going over the derelict garage where you were found. The men who found you were dismantling some engineering lathes next door to take to some new premises they've just rented. You were very lucky.'

'Don't remind me. I keep thinking about it.'

Hamlet touched her hand. 'Sorry, Alix. If you need to talk…?'

Alix held his gaze and burst out laughing. 'You are joking, aren't you? Look what happened last time I confessed my darkest secrets.' She pushed herself further up the bed. 'So, what's the plan for tomorrow?'

'Well, forensics should have finished. They're working through the night because he's in custody. Dependant on what they find, he'll be interviewed about that. And we haven't put to him anything about the five victims yet. Though we did mention Elise, in relation to what happened to her when she was at uni.'

'What did he say about that?'

'Denied it. Says it was someone else who hacked into his accounts.'

'God have mercy.' Alix shook her head. 'So, you didn't mention Elise in terms of her being one of the victims in the bunker?'

'No, we haven't put anything relating to that to him. But to be honest he didn't react as I would have expected him to when her name was brought up. There was no hesitation. His responses, verbal and non-verbal, were very convincing.'

'What are you saying, Hamlet?'

'Clearly he's guilty but his responses were very convincing. He had an answer for every allegation we put to him, with no hesitation whatsoever. I'm going to go home and sleep on it. I've made notes of everything he said, so I'm going to spend a few hours going through everything and see what I can come up with.'

'Need some company for that?'

'You mean you want to come home with me?'

Alix shrugged nonchalantly. 'I've got nothing better to do, and I want to nail the bastard who did this to me. He's got a rape to answer to as well. He's ruined my life. He's not going to get away with that.'

It was 8.30 p.m. before the ward doctor got around to see Alix, and he was more than comfortable with releasing her into Hamlet's care. On their way to the cabin they called in at a curry house and grabbed a takeaway. It was still light when they turned into the clearing. Hamlet left Alix to sort out the food while he took Lucky for a toilet run. Twenty minutes later they were tucking into a Chicken Balti and washing it down with a glass of white wine.

By the time they had finished their meal Alix had drunk three glasses of wine. She leaned back in her chair. 'I'm stuffed, Hamlet.'

Hamlet shook his head. 'Well, seeing as you've been through a traumatic experience you're facing up to it well.'

'That's because I know I'm in the right company if I have a meltdown.' She finished her wine and pushed back her chair. 'Well, shall we get down to business. Show me what you've got. Let's see if we can put this investigation to bed.'

'Everything's in my study,' he answered, rising from the table. He picked up the plates and took them through to the kitchen, dumping them in the sink. Returning, he poured the last of the wine into his and Alix's glasses, handed hers over and led the way to his study.

The moment he switched on the light Alix let out a 'Wow!' He wasn't surprised by her reaction. Paperwork was strewn everywhere. It covered his desk, a spare chair, and was scattered around the floor. Most of the floorspace contained copies of photographs from MIT's incident board. He'd even included Google Maps pictures of the bunker at Low Bradfield and its surrounding area.

Elise Farmer, Molly Fraser, Sophie Booker, Madison Yates, Jessica McKenna and Hayley Stevenson were all lined up in the sequential order they had been abducted, handwritten notes below each one. Above them was a picture of Alix with more notes. Hamlet noticed her eyes lingering over it for several seconds before she took a glug of wine and then lifted her gaze.

'My, you have been busy,' she said. 'Do work know about what happened to me? Have you said anything?'

'No, I haven't said a thing, Alix. No one knows you've shared that with me and it's not come up. I'm presuming you've still not told the boss?'

Alix shook her head. 'No. Not yet. As I've said before the only police that have this information is Cambridgeshire, who investigated. I don't think the detectives who dealt with it even know I'm a cop.'

'Well, you might need to prepare yourself for it coming out,' Hamlet said gently.

'I'll face that hurdle when it comes. For now, I'm keeping shtum.'

Hamlet gave her an understanding nod. 'Well, you'll have the right people around you if that time comes.'

Alix downed the rest of her wine. 'Right, Detective Mottrell, take me through things. Let's see what we can come up with.'

Hamlet dipped down on his haunches and pointed to the photos of the five murdered women. 'I'll go through things in chronological order. From what we know so far, his first victim was your friend Elise. She alleged that someone was stalking her at university and she believed that person was Matthew Denton who was a fellow student on a Journalism Studies course with her. She told you that she had befriended him and spent some time helping him get through his depression.

'At that time Matthew was living with his gran at Shiregreen, and he later rented a room at a house shared by three other people, which included our colleague Nate Fox. Nate told us that Matthew was a quiet individual who kept himself to himself and didn't always stay at the house. It's believed he commuted between his gran's place and the shared house to help her while she was undergoing cancer treatment.

'Elise made a complaint about Matthew to the principal. The emails and stalking on social media continued and Elise made another complaint about Matthew. On this occasion Matthew was suspended and referred for counselling.' Hamlet looked up. 'How am I doing?' he asked Alix.

She gave him a thumbs up. 'You're doing very well for a rookie detective,' she grinned.

He grinned back and returned his gaze to the photographs. 'Matthew goes for counselling. That is with Dr Isobel Casey.' Pausing he added, 'I haven't got a photo of Dr Casey. She's been highlighted as someone we still need to talk to.' He continued, 'Several weeks into the counselling, she receives anonymous greeting cards, silent phone calls and a bunch of flowers left under her windscreen wipers.

'Then Matthew turns up at the same pub where she is drinking with her boyfriend. She is terrified by his actions but she doesn't report him to the police. Instead, she cancels the counselling, refers him to another psychiatrist and transfers to another hospital in her home city. The psychiatrist who picked up Matthew's assessment was none other than Dr Ian Whitton.'

He glanced up, his eyes fixed on Alix. She was fully aware of the relationship between Hamlet and his former colleague. Alix offered up a flabbergasted look and Hamlet returned to his update.

'Ian only had two sessions with Matthew, during which he completely denied his involvement in the allegations made by both Elise and Dr Casey, alleging that he had been set up, and that he believed "someone had it in for him." He repeated the same thing to Katie and me in interview.

'We now know that Matthew decided to leave university, change his name, adopting his mother's maiden name of Ross, and applied to go to Lincoln University where he continued his journalism studies. After graduating he got a job with a paper at Lincoln and then got the post here at Sheffield, working for both *The Star* and the *Sheffield Telegraph*.

'In between all that, eleven years ago you were attacked in your parent's vicarage when you went down there for your summer break from uni. Elise had come down to stay with you, and as I've shared with you, it is now my belief that Elise was the intended target, having continued to be stalked by Matthew Denton.

'I think he followed Elise to your parent's place and lay in wait until that night. As you told me, Elise had got off with a lad down there and didn't get back until after your attack.' He glanced at Alix to see how she was faring. Her mouth was set tight but she gave him a look that told him she was okay.

He continued, 'We know that Elise finished her studies, got a job with a paper in Skipton, close to where her parents lived, met the man who became her husband and bought a house up there. Five years ago Elise disappeared while out walking her dog, and as we know, her body was found a week ago in the bunker at Low Bradfield with our five other victims.' Looking up, he asked, 'Am I still doing okay?'

'We'll make a senior investigative officer of you yet, Hamlet.'

Returning a cocky grin, he visited each of the victims, outlining the date they went missing, describing the nature of their disappearance, the clues left behind, where there were similarities in circumstances prior to each victim's disappearance and finally the discovery of their bodies, with the exception of Hayley Stevenson who was found unconscious but alive.

At this point he raised himself from his crouch, his knees cracking, and perched himself on the edge of his desk, rubbing the back of his legs and stretching them out. 'I've already explained that there is a physical likeness between each of the victims, including you, and there is some similarity in his MO.

'What I haven't told you is that when I made enquiries into Matthew's counselling sessions, I learned that he had been diagnosed with an uncommon disorder called de Clérambault's Syndrome, whereby he is under the delusional belief that an individual is in love with him. He reciprocates that through various means, sending letters and gifts, phoning them and following them. This diagnosis fits in with everything experienced by our victims, including your friend Elise.'

'So, Matthew is definitely our man?'

'Hmmm.'

'That sounds as though you're not sure.'

'I'm almost there, though there are some things that puzzle me about him.'

'In what way?'

'Well, when Elise's name was mentioned to him, I expected some type of reaction. Her name is the only one that the press hasn't speculated as being one of the victims. So only the killer would know that. I gained the impression from what he said, and his demeanour, that he wasn't aware she was dead. He talked about her as if she was alive.

'The other thing I've thought about is where you were found. If we look at the other victims, including Hayley, our killer never intended them to be found. They were hidden in a remote World War Two bunker.

'We know from finding Hayley he had left enough food and water for her to survive for several days, although something appears to have happened that prevented him from returning to her before she was found. It was sheer luck those bunker enthusiasts found her.

'With you, it was a different case. You were left with no food or water at all, and although the garage you were hidden away in was derelict, the premises around you were not. They were all small businesses in operation on almost a daily basis.

'That's been bugging me, and so before I left work, I rang one of the men who found you, and he tells me that for the past week they've been backwards and forwards to the building next door to where you were found stripping out the machinery to move it to their new premises. It wasn't really luck you were found. The moment you called out you were heard.

'Another thing is how forensically aware our killer appears to be. The victims in the bunker were all put in a bath of water and bleach to remove his DNA. And all the surfaces where he had embalmed them were scrupulously clean. And yet the taser he used, the wedding invitations, and the cable ties he used on you, were all found quite easily at his home. They were in his cellar and no effort had been made to hide them.'

'He might not have expected us to find him so quickly,' Alix interposed.

'Maybe. But I don't think our man's that careless. The other thing I haven't told you is that when we spoke to Matthew about your abduction, Katie mentioned that you had received a phone call from him and that he'd called your name when he turned up at your home. He completely denies that. He is adamant he was at home all that night and we've checked his mobile. There is no call to your number.'

'Burner phone?' Alix responded.

'Of course. They're easy enough to get hold of. But forensics haven't found one at his home or his office, and if he'd been as sloppy as the other things we've recovered, I would have expected that phone to be found. Another thing, and what I find interesting, is that he doesn't own a car. Or so he says, and there's not one registered to his name or address. He travels everywhere by public transport. His work colleagues confirm that. Some of them have given him lifts when they've been chasing up stories. So, what I have to ask is, did you actually see Matthew Denton, or Matt Ross, as you know him, the other night? Was it his voice you recognised at the door?'

Alix diverted her eyes to the ceiling in concentration. After several seconds she returned her gaze to Hamlet. 'No, I didn't, to be honest. His voice was muffled. I told Lauren it was Matt Ross only because that's who he said he was. And he seemed to know a lot about Elise. He knew I was her friend from uni, and he told me he needed to talk to me because he had something that might interest me, that would help the investigation.' She put a hand to her mouth. 'My God, Hamlet. Do you think we've got the wrong man?'

Hamlet took a deep breath. 'I can't help but reflect on the answers he gave in the interview. He told both Dr Casey and Dr Whitton — and us — that he believed his social media accounts had been hacked and that he had been set up, and he sounded genuine. There are just too many anomalies for me. I'm not saying he should be released. He certainly needs interviewing again, but before that I'd like to visit his place in the morning and have a look around before we talk to him again. Can you fix that up with the boss?'

TWENTY-TWO

Following an early breakfast, Alix and Hamlet drove over to the street where Matthew Denton lived. His house was a decent sized post-war semi in a large council estate that his gran had bought in the 1980's and had passed on to him after her death. The house had incident tape strung out around its perimeter and a uniformed officer sat in a patrol car by the gate keeping guard and protecting the scene.

Before pulling up, Hamlet drove up and down the road, viewing nearby houses. At the end of the road was a small shopping precinct with many stores selling convenience food, cheap booze and vape cigarettes. Hamlet made a note of these before returning to Matthew's house and parking behind the police car.

The two detectives flashed their ID to the officer, told her they were there to make a couple of enquiries with nearby neighbours, and then locking up the car they set off on foot, Hamlet scouring the fronts of the homes as they ambled along. Five houses along Hamlet spotted what they were looking for. He pointed out to Alix a CCTV camera discreetly positioned beneath the corner guttering of a house, and set off up the drive. As he knocked on the door, he said, 'I've noticed all the shops at the bottom have got CCTV. We'll need to make enquiries there as well.'

Alix looked like she was about to respond when the door was answered. They were greeted by a bespectacled man in his early forties wearing a T-shirt and jeans, and in his stocking-feet. He held a mug of tea that looked freshly brewed. Before they could say anything, he said, 'We've heard Matt's been pulled in over that lass who disappeared and those bodies you've found. Is it true? He's a reporter, you know?'

Hamlet didn't even bother showing his ID. He had to hold back a grin. He didn't think for one minute he looked like a cop and yet that was twice now that he had been identified as one without introducing himself. Had something about him changed? He answered, 'Matthew's helping us with our enquiries and we're just following something up.'

'I've heard all that before,' the man smirked. 'I know quite a few of you lot. I work in security. I get turned out quite regularly by your control room when one of our alarms goes off. How can I help you?'

Hamlet glanced up at the camera on the corner of the house. He suddenly noticed another beside it pointing back towards the garage. And there was one on the garage roof aimed back down the drive. Hamlet pointed to the first one he'd spied. It looked to him as though it had a view to the street in front of the house. 'Your cameras. Are they all operating?' he asked.

'Of course. Fitted them myself. All linked to a hard drive in the house and an app on my phone. I can see anyone coming to the house no matter where I am. You can never be too careful. A few ne'er-do-wells live round here, as if you didn't know. They'd take the coat off your back to fund their habit.'

Hamlet nodded. 'Does that camera up there give you a view on to the footpath?'

'Yep. And the one on the garage looks out on to the road. I know they shouldn't do but no one's complained yet. I've fitted a few houses on this street the same, and I've done a couple of the shops down the bottom. Keeps the toe-rags round here on their toes. We haven't had a break-in on this street for years.'

Hamlet smiled. 'You're just the man we're looking for. Do you mind if we come in and have a look at your system?'

Shortly before midday, armed with a search warrant, Hamlet and Alix drove over to a terraced street in Darnall and met up with a locksmith who got them entry to a house without needing to smash the front door in.

They immediately entered a narrow hallway with a doorway to their left that led into the front room, and a doorway at the end that revealed a steep staircase to the upper two bedrooms and bathroom.

Putting on plastic overshoes and donning latex gloves they separated, Alix taking the upper floors and Hamlet the lower. Remembering his training, Hamlet began at the door and moved right around the outside of the room. The room showed nothing that gave away the age of the property, except for the high ceilings and decorative light rose in the middle of it that shouted late Victorian.

The fireplace had been ripped out and replaced by a wall-mounted fan heater, and the furnishings were contemporary, though the room was untidy, an armchair and part of the sofa spilling over with clothing that looked as if it had been washed but not ironed.

There was an ironing board and iron in the far left corner. On the floor by the sofa was a TV magazine, half bottle of Famous Grouse whisky and an empty glass. On a coffee table in the centre of the room were two closed pizza boxes, the covers grease-stained with whatever the contents had been. The room smelled of stale food.

A large television on a corner unit in the far right corner was the only other thing in the room. Hamlet could see there were few places to hide anything in here, nevertheless he continued to move slowly round, checking. The TV unit contained a number of DVD's, mostly action movies, and a couple of connecting leads. Nothing was behind it or underneath.

The only other places he needed to check was the chair and sofa, and he found nothing around those, so he moved back into the hall and made his way into the kitchen.

He could hear Alix pulling open a drawer up above as he walked past the stairs. The kitchen was also modern in fitment with an arrangement of ivory units and wooden work surfaces, an ivory chalk-painted armoire against the right-hand wall and a central island that had two seats against it.

The worksurfaces were cluttered with opened food packets and dirty pots. More takeaway cartons were on the central island. Hamlet could see very little by way of home cooking going on in this kitchen. Not one pan was anywhere on show.

Once again, he slowly worked his way around the room, searching through the armoire first, moving to the sink and then finally the cupboards. There was nothing of an incriminating nature.

Halfway around the room, in the corner, was a door, and he opened it, expecting to find a larder, and was surprised to see a set of stone steps leading downwards. The house had a cellar.

He found the switch and turned on the light. The walls were whitewashed and looked to be freshly painted. As he made his way down his plastic overshoes rustled on the stone, the sound echoing. At the bottom it opened up to his right. He was heading beneath the hallway and front room, though the proportions looked smaller down in this space.

The walls were again whitewashed and the cellar only contained a large workbench which had an array of tools hung up across the entire back wall. There was a leather high back chair in front of the bench.

Despite the decent looking tools, Hamlet could not see evidence of much work having gone on here. In fact, it was the tidiest workspace he had ever seen. The bench had three cupboards and he opened each door, disappointed to only find boxes of nails and screws, some more electrical leads and a couple of pieces of chain.

He was about to leave and then decided to check the gap beneath, on the off-chance their suspect had dropped or hidden something that would give him away. Lowering himself onto his hands and knees, he dipped his head, manoeuvring into a better position where he could get a closer look. His eyes instantly registered a thin shaft of blue light coming from somewhere behind the bench.

He tried to reach his hand through to feel where it was coming from but couldn't stretch far enough, and so gave one of the legs a tug but it wouldn't shift. Pushing himself up, he skipped up the stone steps, switched off the light and then, slowly this time in the gloom, retraced his steps back down.

On his hands and knees, in the darkness, the blue light was brighter. A decent size shaft of light was creeping out from beneath the workbench giving a blue tinge to the stone floor. He jogged back up the stairs, turned the light back on and shouted upstairs to Alix, 'I've got something.'

She was down in seconds, and on her hands and knees beside Hamlet peering underneath the bench. They tried to pull the workbench away from the wall but it was fastened tight.

Hamlet started to examine the edges, running a finger along the back edge of the bench. As he lowered his eyes, he spotted why they couldn't move it. Two of the legs were longer on the right-hand side and holes had been chiselled into the stone floor, providing a securing slot.

Grabbing the worksurface he heaved it up and half-swinging, half-dragging the bench, he pulled it away from the wall until there was a big enough gap for him to see what was behind. What he saw took him completely by surprise. 'Alix, look at this lot,' he said.

She crowded in behind him to get a better look. In a well organised space was a computer, keyboard, TV monitor and, on a shelf above, a row of several dozen DVDs. Hamlet could see each one had a handwritten spine. He pulled one out.

'Bloody hell!' he exclaimed upon his first look. He turned the plastic box so Alix could get a view. Elise Farmer's name was clearly legible on the spine. The handwriting neat. He leaned in to get a look at the other DVDs. He saw the names of the other victims in the bunker. He opened up the case with Elise's name inscribed. 'Do you want to take a look? See what we've got?' he asked, searching out Alix's eyes.

She returned an uncomfortable look. 'I don't want to, but I know at some stage I'll have to, so let's get it over with.'

Hamlet took out the DVD and loaded the disc into the computer. After a few seconds of whirring a lengthy list of video files appeared on the screen dated in date order. The first date was the day after Elise had gone missing. Following this was daily dates for almost a month, thereafter the dates were weekly and covered a duration of three months. Halfway down the list the video file dates changed to month end, the last of which finished almost fourteen months after Elise's disappearance.

'There's a lot of files on this disc. Shall we look at just a couple?' said Hamlet.

'As I say, I know it's something I'll have to sit through, so no time like the present. I'd rather do it like this, than in briefing. At least only you will see how I react.'

Hamlet clicked on the first video file and the screen revealed a well-lit picture of Elise kneeling up on the same mattress they had found Hayley Stevenson lying on in the War Room. Elise had the same metal clamp around her neck that was chained to the wall, but unlike Hayley she had her hands bound behind her back. Her head was bowed and they could hear she was crying. After a few seconds she looked towards the camera and with tears running over her lips she said softly, 'Why are you doing this? I haven't done anything to you. Please let me go.'

'But you love me,' a man's voice resounded from behind the camera. 'And I love you.'

Hamlet and Alix exchanged a look. The voice sounded familiar. As they returned their eyes to the screen the video footage ended with a close-up of Elise's face. She looked bewildered.

'Do you want to look at another one?' Hamlet asked, scrolling down the list.

'I don't have a choice. I need to,' Alix replied, tight-mouthed.

Hamlet selected one of the dates from the month end list. This one was in October of the first year of her disappearance. The moment he clicked on the file a close-up of Elise's face appeared. They could clearly see she had lost weight, with gaunt cheekbones, and she looked sleep-deprived with dark-rimmed eyes. There were no tears this time, instead she looked angry.

'Fuck off!' she yelled. 'Why are you doing this? How many times do I have to tell you, I don't love you! Now let me go and that will be the end of it. I promise I won't tell anyone.'

The man behind the camera let out a laugh.

'You know what, you're fucking sick,' Elise shouted and made an attempt at lashing out. The camera wobbled and then the footage ended.

Hamlet looked to Alix again. 'You okay?'

She nodded. 'Poor Elise. She probably wouldn't have known then she was going to die.'

Hamlet hovered the curser over the last video file. 'Do you want to see the last one?'

'Let's get it over with.'

The file opened up on Elise, dressed in the wedding dress they had found her in, tied to one of the chairs in the War Room. She was pleading, 'Why are you doing this, for God's sake? I've told you I'm not going to say anything. I'll do anything you want. Just let me go now, I've been here long enough.'

Suddenly a dark shadow blotted out the screen for several seconds, then the legs and torso of someone dressed in black walked towards Elise. More of the figure was revealed as it got closer to her, and as the person slipped behind the chair Elise was tied to, they could see that the man was wearing latex gloves and a black masquerade mask.

Hamlet and Alix shot a gaze at one another. For a second, they held each other's look, and Hamlet was about to comment on the man's disguise when Elise's terrified scream whipped their eyes back to the monitor. They were just in time to see him placing a transparent plastic bag over her head, muffling her cries.

'Jesus!' Alix gasped.

Hamlet never let his eyes drift. He watched as the man pulled the bag fully over Elise's head, tightening its drawstring around her neck. At that moment Hamlet realised the bag he was using was an exit hood people bought over the internet when they wanted to undertake euthanasia and he couldn't start to imagine what was going through Elise's mind.

She started to thrash and the man clasped his hands around her head, pressing his elbows down on her shoulders to restrain her. A look of abject terror masked Elise's face as the plastic started to mould around her head. Her face turned red as she sucked, the plastic tightening around her lips, but that only lasted seconds as a blue tinge washed over her mouth.

The rasping noise she made as she fought for air made the hairs on Hamlet's neck and arms stand up. Suddenly, her eyes rolled back, only the whites showing, and seconds later her head flopped forward onto her chest. She was dead. It had taken just over a minute.

'The bastard!' Alix exclaimed.

'I know now why none of the victims showed marks of violence. He suffocated them,' Hamlet responded.

'Fourteen months he kept Elise. And then he did that to her. The fucking bastard.' Taking a deep breath, Alix added, 'We need to contact the boss. She needs to see this. And we need to get CSI here.'

TWENTY-THREE

Later that day, carrying handfuls of exhibit bags, and a folder full of still images taken from the seized DVDs, Hamlet and Alix strolled into a warm and stuffy interview room at the custody suite. Already there, seated next to his federation solicitor was Detective Nathaniel Fox.

Nate looked around as they entered, aiming a hateful stare at Alix. 'Here she is. My once upon a time partner, now prepared to stab me in the back for more promotion.'

Alix held back from what she wanted to say, maintaining a straight face as she eased herself down in a seat opposite. She organised her folder, glanced momentarily at the notes she had prepared for this interview, and then turned her eyes to Hamlet. He gave her an encouraging nod. One that said 'you can do this'.

'This is crazy, Alix,' Nate said. 'You've arrested me for abducting and murdering the women in the bunker. There is a mistake. I'm working on the case myself to try and find their killer. My DNA must have somehow contaminated the evidence.' Then he aimed a stare at Hamlet. 'Or has the doc managed to persuade you again? I bet this is all his doing.'

Alix fixed her gaze onto her former partner. 'We'll explain everything, Nate, as we go along, and then you can have your say.' She glanced up towards the corner of the ceiling where the video camera was, its green light showing. In the room next door, Lauren and a couple of her colleagues would be watching and listening. 'Shall we start then?'

'This is a big mistake, Alix,' Nate responded.

'Let me first begin by telling you what happened this morning. Detective Mottrell and myself went to the street where Matt Ross, or should I say Matthew Denton, lives, and conducted some door-to-door enquiries. As you know, Matthew was arrested for the abduction of Hayley Stevenson, and the abduction and murder of five other women whose bodies were found in a disused World War Two bunker at Low Bradfield. Some of the things he said in interview made us take another approach to our enquiry. Notably that he had been set up by someone, and that the taser, plastic ties, and wedding invitations we found at his home had been planted.

'We decided to check if that could be true and so we went to his home to see if anyone on that street had CCTV fitted that would provide us with evidence to corroborate what he said.' She noted an immediate change in Nate's look. 'We looked at footage stored on the hard drives of two nearby houses, and we discovered that whilst Matthew was at work someone paid a visit to his home. Do you know who that someone was, Nate?'

'Enlighten me.'

'It was you, Nate.' From a folder she slipped out one of the stills she had taken from the security officer's CCTV system. It showed Nate in his suit and tie heading in the direction of Matthew's home. There was no mistaking who it was. She pulled out another still. This was found on another neighbour's CCTV, who lived opposite, and showed Nate heading up Matthew's drive to the back. 'Would you agree that's you?' she asked.

He shrugged.

'What were you doing there?'

'Making enquiries.'

'On your own?'

'I had a hunch. I didn't want to look a fool. Remember I knew him from my university days. He'd behaved oddly with Elise and that psychiatrist he was referred to. And he'd been diagnosed with that syndrome the doc here mentioned. I thought he might be worth checking out. I didn't know if he would be at work or not.'

'But how did you know where he lived? We hadn't discovered Matthew Denton was in fact Matt Ross when these images captured you going to his house. We found that out later that day.'

For a second, he didn't respond, then he answered, 'When I saw him at the press conference, I thought I recognised him. I did a quick check of the electoral register and found out where he lived. It wasn't difficult.'

Alix released a smile. 'You recovered very quickly there, Nate. Your years of being a detective have stood you in good stead.'

'I don't know what you mean. I just had to think things through. I was acting on my initiative and I didn't mention this at briefing because I wasn't sure I'd got it right.'

'So, when you discovered where Matthew lived and went down there, why didn't you call it in and why didn't you tell anyone? And why didn't you record it anywhere? You know that's the procedure.'

'I didn't need to. It all came out at briefing about his identity and I didn't want to take the limelight.'

Alix couldn't help but release another grin. 'You're good at this. Do you know that?'

'Don't know what you mean.'

'So, these CCTV images we've got then from neighbours don't show you sneaking into Matthew Denton's house three days ago and planting items in there?'

'Absolutely not. I went to his house on a hunch and to get the lie of the land. I was going to bring it up at briefing but was beaten to it. Why would I do that?'

'Because you wanted to blame Matthew for the abduction and murders, when in fact it was you who abducted and killed them,' Alix snapped back.

Beneath the table Hamlet tapped her ankle gently with his foot.

Alix nodded. 'Detective Mottrell, would you turn over exhibit one please?'

Hamlet turned over the evidence bag. Inside was one of the DVD cases they had recovered from Nate's hiding place behind the workbench.

Careful to display no emotion, Alix said, 'Early this afternoon, Detective Mottrell and I executed a warrant at your home, and in your cellar, behind a false wall, we discovered a computer and several DVDs. The DVDs contained video footage of Elise Farmer, Molly Fraser, Sophie Booker, Madison Yates and Jessica McKenna in the bunker, where they were recently found, being murdered. This one contains evidence of Elise's horrific murder. Your first victim. What have you to say about that?'

TWENTY-FOUR

The celebrations in the pub were anything but a celebration. The mood among the MIT team was extremely subdued. A few held court at the bar, but the majority were sat at tables, in clusters, drinking sombrely. There was no celebratory speech by Lauren or talk of bringing about a successful conclusion to a disturbing investigation because they knew this was going to have terrible repercussions for years to come.

Not only had they uncovered that a cop was the serial killer they had been hunting, but he was one of their own detectives. There would be horrendous headlines, a public outcry and certainly a government inspection of the force following this. There would be accusations of a cover-up, speculation over what colleagues and management knew about Detective Nathaniel Fox. Another force would surely be brought in to investigate and scrutinise the work of the department. Everyone was going to be under the spotlight.

'That's the hardest interview I've ever done. I never want to repeat it again,' Alix said, nursing her glass of wine. She had hardly drunk in the ten minutes she had been sat with Hamlet.

'You handled it very well, Alix. That was a very difficult interview and the way you kept your emotions in check, you deserve a medal. You had to sit and watch through that DVD of what he did to your friend Elise. And also, I'm guessing you were also thinking about what he probably did to you as well.'

'I couldn't stop thinking about that, all the time he was talking. I just kept thinking why don't I recognise your voice. I thought I would have done, but I didn't. Maybe it wasn't Nate who raped me.'

'It was eleven years ago. You were nineteen. It was a very traumatic incident. The likelihood is that you've blotted most of it out. People do. That's how we cope in order to get on with life. I have my own struggles at times, trying to recall what happened that day Helen and our baby were murdered and I was left for dead. All I remember was the look on her face when I walked in from the garden. She was sat at the kitchen table and I knew something was up, but that's all I remember, until I woke up in the hospital with you scowling down at me.'

'If it's any consolation, your case also ran through my mind while I was interviewing Nate. I was wrong about you. I kept thinking, have I got it wrong about Nate?'

Hamlet reached across to her. 'You didn't get it wrong, Alix. Those videos prove Nate did what he did to those women. Nate is a killer, who covered up who he really is extremely well. He made Matthew Denton the fall guy when they were at uni. My guess is that it was him who hacked into Matthew's accounts to cover his tracks. The same with Dr Casey. We now know it was Nate who invited Matthew to the pub on the occasion she was there with her boyfriend. Poor Matthew. He had to change his name and move away because of the embarrassment of what people believed about him. It will be interesting to see the headlines he writes.'

'No, it won't. I'm praying he won't name me, or any of us. There's a shit-storm coming our way as it is.'

'He'll not name names. The paper's legal team won't allow that.'

A shadow loomed over them and they both looked up. It was Lauren.

She said, 'I'm just saying cheerio to everyone. I've just taken a call. The Chief's called me in. "Strategy meeting." I'd best take my stab jacket and tin hat. Something tells me it's going to be a teeny bit uncomfortable in there.' She exhaled deeply. 'Before I go, I want to give you two my personal thanks. That was a great piece of detective work. But it's only the start. I'm not the only one thinking there might be more bodies out there. There's a lot of digging needs to be done because Nate certainly isn't the person we thought he was. I think this business in the bunker is only the tip of the iceberg.'

Alix and Hamlet exchanged a grim look. Hamlet's first case as a detective certainly hadn't been a straightforward one.

A NOTE TO THE READER

Dear Reader,

Coming up with the character of Dr Hamlet Mottrell and pitching the idea to my publisher to start a new series featuring him was the easy part, particularly because he is based on a real forensic psychiatrist with a fascinating job in a secure unit, and I had his first outing in *See Them Die* in the early stages of development.

The difficulty came with this follow-up book. The question I asked myself, as I set about creating the storyline, was how could I push the boundaries of Hamlet into storylines that would see him frequently chasing down serial killers without them sounding unrealistic or ridiculous? And by good fortune, my question was answered thanks to the Home Office announcing the fast-track recruitment of people to become detectives without the need to be uniformed constables. After all, Hamlet already had the skills of dealing with psychopaths and serial offenders, he just needed the right environment to thrive, and so this book took on a whole new lease of life. Progressing the development of Hamlet through further adventures is no longer daunting for me. Book three is well under way and book four has gone beyond the idea stage.

Before I close there are some thanks. First, to Amy Durant for her editing skills. I cannot thank her enough for her continued labours. She makes my story sing. Also, a big shout to the Sapere Books team who are just the friendliest and most supportive bunch of people. They also work closely with their authors to come up with some terrific covers. They produced some amazing ones for my Hunter Kerr series, but the one for

See Them Die and this one are beyond superb. And, as I write this, I have just seen the third cover for the third Hamlet book, which is out later this year – it's a belter.

I also want to thank the reviewers and my readers. You have reacted wonderfully to *See Them Die*, writing some very endearing reviews that have helped launch another fictional

Lastly, I thank you the reader, and all the book bloggers and reviewers who have left such kind reviews. Word of mouth is such a powerful thing and without you I would have fewer readers, so, if you have enjoyed this book, would you kindly leave a review on **Amazon** or **Goodreads**. And, if you want to contact me, or want me to appear and give a talk about my writing journey at one of the groups you belong to, then please feel free to do so through **my website**.

Thank you for reading.

Michael Fowler

www.mjfowler.co.uk

Sapere Books is an exciting new publisher of brilliant fiction and popular history.

To find out more about our latest releases and our monthly bargain books visit our website:
saperebooks.com

Printed in Great Britain
by Amazon